THE GIRL IN THE WHISPERS

DAVID K. WILSON

Copyright © 2024 by David K. Wilson
All rights reserved.
ISBN-13: 978-1-7333457-8-1

Cover design by Caroline Johnson
Author photo by Mallory Wilson

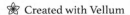 Created with Vellum

1

CATHERINE DROVE down the dark road, her car's headlights slicing through the black night. She glanced at the rear-view mirror to check on six-year-old Sarah, who slept peacefully in the back seat. Too big for a traditional child's car seat but still small enough to need a booster seat, Sarah's blonde hair fell over her face as she leaned against a pillow she had wedged up to the window. Catherine smiled at her daughter's preciousness and looked back at the road, shaking her head back and forth to stay awake. She'd already been driving for three hours but was less than a half hour from home.

If she were alone, she would have blasted the radio to stay awake, but she wanted Sarah to be able to sleep. She also would've cracked a window for fresh air, but it had begun to rain. Instead, she stretched the muscles in her face, chuckling at the thought of Sarah giggling at the funny faces she was probably making.

As the rain fell harder, she slowed down and squinted, trying to focus on the yellow lines that rushed past her in the middle of the road. She glanced back to Sarah and her heart stopped.

The back seat was empty.

Panic surged through Catherine's body.

"Sarah? SARAH?"

She turned to look for her daughter, but she was nowhere to be seen. And then she heard her voice, crying out in terror.

"Mommy!"

Catherine woke with a jolt, adjusting in the passenger seat. Her husband, Dale, glanced over from the driver's seat.

"You okay?" he asked.

Catherine nodded and smiled weakly.

"I guess I dozed off for a minute," she replied quietly.

"A minute?" Dale said with a sly grin. "You've been out for at least an hour."

Catherine nodded, not completely surprised. She turned her gaze out the window and watched the forest of cypress and oak trees rush past her as they drove through the thick, swampy Louisiana backwoods. She leaned her forehead against the window and traced her fingers over the faded crayon scribbles on the door panel.

"I appreciate you coming with me," Dale said, reaching out to squeeze her left hand.

Catherine squeezed back then wrestled her hand away, unconsciously covering the scar on her wrist.

"Your father needs help," she said. "I understand. You're the only family he has left."

Dale scoffed. "It's just bad timing is all. And I know

you didn't want to come. I just didn't think you should be left alone."

"God forbid I be unsupervised for a minute," Catherine replied.

"You know what I mean," Dale said with a sigh. "Just with everything..."

"I'm not going to try and kill myself again, Dale," Catherine said.

"Jeez, Cat."

The two drove on in an uncomfortable silence until Dale finally got up the nerve to finish his thought.

"Maybe this will be good for us," Dale said, opting for a different subject. "A change of scenery might help."

Catherine turned back toward the window, rejecting his suggestion.

A change of scenery might help? she thought. *Is he that naive?*

But she softened quickly, reminding herself that he was trying his best. Although she didn't turn her gaze away from the passing trees, she reached over to hold his hand.

2

THE JEEP WRANGLER turned off the single lane road and trundled down a meandering gravel driveway that cut through the woods. The trees eventually cleared, and Catherine saw the dilapidated Gothic country mansion that had nearly been swallowed by time, neglect and the surrounding swamp. At one time, the house had clearly been an elegant and luxurious structure, but now, ivy and Spanish moss crawled through every shadowy nook and cranny of the decaying monstrosity.

"I guess he fired the groundskeeper," Dale quipped.

"This is where you grew up?" Catherine asked as she sat up in her seat.

"Only until he sent me away to boarding school," Dale replied. "I guess it's been in the family for generations. Leave it to Henry to run it into the ground."

"I can't believe you never told me," she said. "Or brought me here."

"Trust me," Dale said. "I did you a favor."

"Are you nervous about seeing your dad?" Catherine asked.

"I fully expect for him to be a total asshole," Dale said.

"The last time we saw him, we didn't exactly part on the best of terms," Catherine replied.

"Trust me. He made me very aware of that when I called to tell him we were coming."

"Then why are we even here?" she asked.

"Like you said. I'm the only family he's got. I promise we won't stay long. Just make sure he's all situated."

The Jeep turned into the circular driveway and pulled to a stop in front of the house. A massive oak door was framed by huge, ivy-covered pillars on a rotting porch. Dale stared at it, feeling the wave of a thousand memories.

"I don't know if I can do this," he mumbled.

"There's no place like home," Catherine said.

Just as Dale cracked his car door, the front door of the house opened.

A disheveled man appeared out of the darkness on a motorized wheelchair. Henry Devereux was a severe looking man in his early 70s. He held a permanent scowl on his face and a glass of bourbon in his right hand.

"Shit," Dale muttered as he stepped out of the car.

He and Catherine walked carefully up the creaking steps and greeted their host with polite smiles.

"You're early," he griped in a slow, Southern drawl.

A woman stepped out of the shadows behind Henry and smiled warmly at Catherine.

"We made good time," Dale replied. "Hope that's okay."

"Don't seem like I have much of a choice," Henry replied, turning his attention to Catherine.

"Catherine, my dear. Are you doing okay?"

"Hello, Henry," Catherine said.

"I consider it nothing short of a miracle that you're even here," Henry replied.

"Don't start, Henry," Dale said.

Henry looked at his son to let him know he realized he was being disrespected.

"Well, alright then," he said, turning his wheelchair around and heading back in the house. "I need another drink. Dale, you know your way around."

Dale turned to Catherine and shrugged.

"Home sweet home," he said. "I'll grab the bags."

Catherine nodded and turned her attention to the woman still standing in the doorway.

"Hi. I'm Catherine, Dale's wife," she said.

The woman nodded. Her dark hair was pulled up under a colorful scarf that complimented her caramel skin and brought even more attention to her gentle green eyes and warm smile. Catherine immediately liked her.

"I apologize for Mr. Henry. He isn't much for introductions," she said, the words rolling over Creole accent. "I'm Delphine. I help take care of Mr. Personality and keep the house in order."

Catherine couldn't help but notice the withering porch.

"I focus on the inside," Delphine said with a wink.

3

CATHERINE PAUSED to adjust her eyes to the darkness. The deep mahogany wood paneling and heavy tapestries seemed to swallow what little light managed to find its way into the large foyer.

The house seemed frozen in another time. The foyer was cluttered with porcelain knickknacks, ornate decorations and antique furnishings, all draped in untold history. A massive staircase curved upstairs, its dark and heavy banister serving as a guard rail to the open hallway of the second floor.

Catherine noticed several old photographs hung near the staircase and walked closer to study them. One of the frames hung askew and she reached out to straighten it, studying the black and white image of a group of people gathered at what appeared to be a picnic.

"Maybe Dale can shed some light on these photos," Delphine said. "Henry refuses to speak about them."

Catherine glanced at another frame, her breath

catching. It was a picture of a young boy dressed in a fireman's helmet and wearing a red towel as a cape.

"Oh, my God," Catherine said.

"Oh, great," Dale said, walking up behind her. "Now you know my true identity."

"I thought that was you," Catherine said, tracing the edge of the picture.

"It WAS me," Dale replied.

"You had Sarah's nose," Catherine said, her words trailing off with her thoughts.

"Y'all just gonna waste the day looking at the past?" Henry's Louisiana twang cut through the air as he wheeled up behind them.

Dale spun around to his father, like a child caught doing something he shouldn't.

"Where should I put our things?" he asked.

"Second floor is all yours," Henry replied, patting the armrest of his wheelchair. "I don't get up there as much lately."

"Ms. Catherine, let me help," Delphine offered.

"I'll get these," Dale said, picking up the bags and walking past his wife.

He nodded toward his dad.

"Maybe Henry can show you around the house."

"You go ahead, dear," Delphine said. "I'll help Dale."

"Henry, would that be alright?" Catherine asked.

Henry let out a deep, weary, overdramatic sigh and motioned for her to follow him.

"Come on," he grumbled.

After taking the bags up to his old bedroom, Dale returned to the Jeep for the rest of their belongings. He yanked out a large duffel bag that was wedged in the back, then froze. Hidden behind it was a box he had not expected to find.

4

CATHERINE FOLLOWED Henry into the parlor. Even with the white oak blinds of the bay windows pulled shut, the room was markedly brighter than the rest of the house. Henry maneuvered past a maroon leather couch and matching recliner, their surfaces worn and creased like the face of an old man, to a beautiful Tiffany lamp sitting on a small table. He yanked on the chain several times to turn the light on and the light flickered on and off in response.

"Cursed lamp," he grumbled. "Been a pain in my ass for decades."

Finally, the lamp cooperated, and the bulb's glow illuminated the room.

"There we go," he said.

He turned around and gave a disinterested wave as he wheeled through the room.

"This is the parlor," he said. "Or sitting room. Or drinking room. Pick your own poison."

He pointed across the hallway to another room.

"And the kitchen's right through there."

Catherine followed him as he led her toward the kitchen, but stopped when Dale walked in, carrying a cardboard box with the word SARAH scrawled on it.

"Cat?" he said gently, holding up the box.

Catherine tried to take the box from him, but he held it away.

"It's just a few things," she said.

"Hon, we talked about this," Dale said.

"You talked about it," Catherine said. "It's not hurting anything."

"We need to put some distance between this. Just temporarily. That's why we're here."

"That's why YOU'RE here," Catherine said, reaching again for the box.

"That's not fair," Dale said, not giving it up. "You're not in this alone."

He stopped himself when he noticed Henry had turned to watch. Dale pulled Catherine aside and the couple began to argue in loud whispers.

"I can't just pretend she never existed," Catherine said.

"No one is asking you to," Dale replied. "But you can't keep feeding your grief."

"You think I want to feel this way?" Catherine said. "You can't understand."

"She was my daughter, too," Dale said, clenching his jaw.

Catherine's eyes began to fill with tears, and Dale reached out to console her, But Catherine yanked away.

"You don't know the guilt," she said. "You couldn't know."

Dale nodded, knowing nothing he said would be right.

He turned and walked away with the box while Catherine watched helplessly. Only then did she become aware of Henry sitting there, taking it all in. She quickly wiped the tears from her eyes and put on a brave face. Henry shook the ice in his glass.

"Who needs a drink?" he said, as he turned and headed back towards the kitchen.

5

After Henry finished his lackluster "tour" of the downstairs, Dale joined them. Catherine seized the opportunity to get a break from the curmudgeon, suggesting the two men had a lot of catching up to do and rushing away before either could protest.

She walked up the stairs where the decorative wooden rail continued along one side of the long landing, exposing it the foyer below. Along the other side were several doors. Catherine looked down the dark hallway that extended further into darkness. She looked for a light switch, but there didn't appear to be one, so she turned her attention back to the doors, one of which was cracked open.

She entered and immediately knew it was Dale's childhood room. A recurring character seemed to dominate the decor: an animated Dalmatian wearing a fire helmet. A poster of the dog hung behind the full-size bed's headboard with bold red letters that proudly read FIREDOG FRED.

Catherine picked up a stuffed animal of the dog and sat down on the Firedog Fred bedspread. Something familiar caught her eye. It was Sarah's box, sitting on top of the tall white dresser. A slip of paper was sitting on top of it.

Catherine stood to read the note.

"I'm an idiot. Please forgive me. I love you. Dale."

Catherine felt a wave of gratitude wash over her. Both for the box and for her husband. Since Sarah's death, they had both been struggling in their own way. Dale's inclination seemed to be denial. Or was he just trying to help pull Catherine out of the depression that seemed to be swallowing her? Then, every once in a while, he'd do something like this and it would remind her that he was struggling with how to handle things, just like her.

Catherine sat the note down on the dresser and picked up the box, setting it down on the bed and kneeling in front of it as she opened it.

It was filled with keepsakes. Crayon drawings, including a piece of light blue construction paper with three stick figures, each labeled with crude lettering, "Mom," "Dad," and "Me." There were also random keepsakes that would have had little meaning to anyone else, like a jar of sand that Catherine knew was from Sarah's first visit to a beach. There were also pictures. Catherine picked up a small, framed photo and looked at the beautiful 5-year-old girl with a beaming smile and short blonde hair.

Tears welled in her eyes and a single drop landed on the construction paper, creating a dark circle. Catherine tried to dab it dry and put the paper out of harm's way.

And then she heard something. It began as a faint, barely audible whisper, and then it grew louder. Catherine shook her head.

No. Not again.

She clenched her eyes shut to make it go away, but the whispering only grew louder. It was several voices jumbled together so she couldn't make out what they were saying. She could feel her heart pounding and she struggled to breathe. She shook her head and hit her ears violently. Anything to make the whispers go away. Instead, she also began to hear the steady, piercing banging of metal on metal. It grew louder and louder.

Catherine tried to remember the exercises they had taught her at the treatment center. She tried to force deep breaths, which began to calm her enough that she looked around the room for a plausible explanation. And then she found it.

Along the far wall, a radiator hissed and clanked.

Catherine let out a heavy sigh of relief. Tears and laughter mixed as she wiped her eyes and regained her composure. The sound of footsteps lumbering up the stairs brought her fully back into reality and she wiped the tears as she closed the box and stood just as Dale entered the room.

"Hey, listen," he said. "About earlier."

Catherine stopped him.

"The note summed it up perfectly. You're an idiot."

She smiled at him, letting him know she accepted his apology.

"How's the reunion?" she asked.

"It has not been a Hallmark moment," Dale replied.

"I'm sure it will just take time," Catherine said.

"Not sure how long it takes to melt a lifetime of ice," Dale replied with a sigh.

He sat down on the edge of the bed and Catherine sat next to him.

"So, what do you think of my old room?" Dale said, trying to lighten the mood.

Catherine grabbed a stuffed Firedog Fred off the bed.

I thought you were sixteen when you left," she said. "Did you have a hard time growing up?"

"Yeah, these are the last remnants of me before he shipped me off to boarding school," Dale explained. "After that, I was just home for summers and didn't really care."

"I don't think I saw a single picture of your mom anywhere," she said.

Dale chuckled.

"Henry doesn't like the reminders," he said. "Or 'won't allow any wallowing in the past.'"

He took the stuffed animal from Catherine and scooted a little closer.

"You know, I never had a girl in my room before."

Catherine leaned away to avoid his advances. "Really? That's so surprising."

Dale caressed Catherine's arm and turned her face toward him, kissing her gently on the lips.

Catherine pulled away. Dale let out a sigh.

"I'm sorry," Catherine said.

Dale smiled and nodded.

"It's okay," he said with a wink. "I told you I'd be

patient. And I will. It's just that damn firedog gets me so turned on."

6

CLAIMING the oven hasn't worked in years, Henry insisted they order pizza for dinner that night, and further insisted Dale go pick it up as no one would actually deliver to their home out in the middle of nowhere.

Dale wanted to argue. The last thing he wanted to do was get back in the car, drive all the way into town, pick up food and drive back. He thought he was done driving for the day. But Catherine urged him to go along with it. And, about an hour later, they all sat around the dining table, lit only by candles.

"Do you ever turn on any lights?" Dale asked.

"Why would I want to pay money just so I can see what I've already seen?" Henry asked back. "Besides, it sets a mood."

Delphine had asked to be excused from dinner. She wanted to take advantage of other people keeping an eye on Henry and finally get a little sleep. However, as everyone was finishing up, she came back in the room.

"I guess my body plain ol' forgot how to sleep," she said with a smile.

She noticed Catherine hadn't eaten much of her pizza.

"Is that pizza okay, Ms. Catherine?" She asked. "I can whip you up something else."

Dale turned to his wife.

"Honey, are you okay?"

"I'm fine," Catherine answered. "I'm just not that hungry."

"Good food is good for the soul," Henry said, his words rolling around in a slight slur.

Delphine laughed.

"That's what I say to you when you don't eat," she said to the old man. "Glad to see you listen sometimes."

Delphine and Catherine laughed, as Henry just ignored the comment and reached for another slice of pepperoni pizza.

"Laugh all you want," he said. "I'm gonna have more pizza."

He took a bite and pulled the slice away, creating a long string of melted cheese from his mouth to the pizza.

"So, Catherine," he finally said, after chewing loudly. "You still hearing voices?"

"Jesus!" Dale exclaimed. "Are you serious?"

Henry leaned back, shocked that the question could have offended anyone.

"What? You're the one who told me," Henry said.

"The medicine helps," Catherine answered calmly. The question had admittedly shaken her for a second, but she actually appreciated the candidness. Dale refused to even acknowledge Catherine's breakdown, much less talk about it. But she decided not to mention the day's earlier episode.

Henry studied her, unsure whether to believe her or not. Finally, he nodded and downed his bourbon, shaking the glass tumbler of ice.

"You're right about that. Medicine definitely helps," he said. "And it looks like I need a refill of my prescription."

Henry rolled into the parlor to grab a fresh bottle of bourbon and Dale stormed after him.

"What the hell was that?" he asked, standing between his father and the liquor cart.

"What are you talking about?" Henry asked. "Get out of my way."

"I know you're not as oblivious as you make yourself out to be," Dale said.

"What are you saying, boy?" Henry glared. "Spit it out."

"Can you try to be a little sensitive? For once?"

"I'm not gonna tip-toe around the obvious," Henry replied. "She didn't seem to be bothered by it. Now get out of my way."

Dale stood his ground.

"Why do you have to be this way?" he asked.

"What way?" Henry demanded, clearly annoyed. "Just because I'm not Mr. Sensitive? You're one to talk."

"We lost a child," Dale said. "I nearly lost my wife. You know what? This was a mistake. We shouldn't have come. We're leaving in the morning."

Henry stared at him, searching for the right thing to say.

"What about the ramp?" he finally asked.

Dale had promised Henry he'd build him a wheelchair-accessible ramp out the front and side doors.

"I ordered all the lumber like you asked," Henry continued. "You want me to return it?"

Dale let out a sigh. "Fine. I'll build your damn ramps. Just try not to be such an asshole."

He walked around his father and back to the dining room.

"Try not to be such a baby," Henry grumbled under his breath.

7

AN HOUR LATER, after the men had retreated to opposite ends of the house in a display of what was probably their father/son dynamic most of their lives, Catherine and Delphine were left to clean up.

"He's actually harmless," Delphine said, as she scrubbed a plate with a rag before dipping it in rinse water. "Living alone all these years has worn down his filter."

"It's okay," Catherine replied, taking the plate and drying it with a hand towel. "Honestly, I prefer it to being tip-toed around."

Delphine nodded and smiled.

"Where is your family?" she asked.

"I'm an only child and my parents passed away a few years ago."

"I'm sorry to hear that," Delphine said.

The two women cleaned in silence for a moment, until Delphine got the nerve to ask her next question.

"Henry said you lost your daughter. In a car accident?"

Catherine nodded. She could feel the always-present hollowness in her heart grow.

"Sarah," she said, her voice cracking.

"I don't mean to pry. I'm sorry," Delphine said gently. "But if you ever want to talk about it –"

She glanced at the scars on Catherine's wrists.

"Or about anything – just know that I'm here."

"Thank you, Delphine. I appreciate it," Catherine replied with a gentle smile. "I mean, Dale is trying. But he walks on eggshells around me. And I know he... I know he blames me."

"That's not true."

"He's never said it and I'm sure he'd deny it, but he has to. I blame me. It was my fault."

"Henry said you fell asleep at the wheel?"

"I nodded out for a half- second. And then..." her voice trailed off as she lost herself in the memory, but then she quickly pulled herself together. "I'd rather not talk about it, if you don't mind."

"Of course," Delphine said. "Just know I'm here. I know it's probably hard to talk to Dale. He's suffering in his own way. And Henry... Well, Henry has his own demons. I'm a friendly, non-partial ear if you ever need one."

Catherine smiled at her new friend.

"I'm so glad you're here," she said. "If I was stuck in this house alone with those two men, I don't know how I'd cope."

"Trust me. I know the feeling."

The two women smiled and, for a brief moment, Catherine didn't feel alone for the first time in a very long time.

CATHERINE DROVE down the dark road, her car's headlights slicing through the black night. She glanced at the rear-view mirror to check on six-year-old Sarah, who slept peacefully in the back seat.

As it began to rain, she quickly rolled the window up, surprised at the sudden downpour. Sheets of rain began to fall, and while her wiper blades did their best to slap it away, it became difficult to see.

And then she heard Sarah's terrified voice.

"Mommy!"

Before she could react, the car hit something, throwing Catherine forward. Darkness swallowed her and then icy water began pouring in all around her. Catherine struggled against her seat belt, but it refused to release her.

"SARAH!"

The car filled rapidly, and Catherine struggled relentlessly to stay above the rising water. As it rose above her head, Catherine leaned back, gasping for one last breath before she was completely submerged.

As she held her breath, hoping for a miracle but expecting the worst, she saw something. Her car's headlights cast eerie beams of light through the water, and something floated in front of her. A dark silhouette of a little girl. Catherine's heart pounded in her ears as the shape morphed into a swirling black cloud, expanding and moving toward her. Catherine screamed, bubbles escaping her lips as the black cloud engulfed her.

She jolted awake with a gasp; her body drenched in sweat. Propping herself up on her elbows, she turned to see Dale sleeping soundly beside her. A sliver of moonlight snuck into the bedroom, casting a blue-gray light that trailed across the bed and up the dresser to Sarah's box.

She lay back down and began to silently cry.

UNABLE TO SLEEP, Catherine watched the room slowly brighten to the morning sun. When Dale's phone alarm went off, her heart sank. She wasn't ready to talk to anyone, much less put on a brave face to greet the day. Every morning was the same struggle. All she wanted to do was hide in bed, away from other people. But she knew that would only draw more concern and attention. Instead, she shut her eyes and pretended to sleep as Dale got dressed for his routine morning run.

She waited until she was sure he was gone, and then listened for other signs of life. Confident everyone else was still asleep, she pulled herself out of bed and went downstairs.

After making a pot of coffee, she retreated to the parlor where the first thing she did was open the window blinds to let in the morning sun. To her delight, the bay windows overlooked a large yard.

While it was currently overrun with ivy and weeds, it was apparent that someone had taken great care of it at one time. Tall unruly hedges created natural privacy boundaries on either side of the house. Toppled statues and what looked to be a decorative fountain had also been consumed by nature. Still, natural beauty emerged in the decay. Yellow and white wildflowers brought delicate splashes of color to the yard and the early morning sun caught reflections on the morning dew.

Catherine sat on the couch and sipped her coffee, savoring the peaceful beauty. Lost in non-thought, an hour passed by before she knew it. She was finally nudged back to the real world when she heard the kitchen door open. She turned to see her husband walking into the room, dressed in shorts and a T-shirt drenched with sweat from a morning run. He kissed Catherine on the forehead and they both looked out the windows.

"It's really gorgeous out there," he said. "A little break in the humidity. You should get out and go for a walk before it gets unbearable again."

"I'm fine in here," Catherine said. She spoke so quietly it was almost a whisper.

"Well, at least turn a light on," Dale said.

He pulled the chain on the Tiffany lamp, unsuccessfully trying to turn it on. He laughed.

"He still hasn't fixed this thing," he said.

"It's beautiful," Catherine said.

"Wasted on that old blowhard," Dale said. "He never liked it."

"Then why does he keep it?" she asked. "Henry doesn't strike me as a sentimental type."

Dale replied something about it being his mother's

favorite lamp, but Catherine was only half listening. A movement near the back of the yard had caught her attention. She looked harder. She felt certain she had seen a young girl, about five or six, in a yellow dress. She would appear in the gaps between a series of small shrubs as she chased a butterfly. The morning shadows made it hard to really see, but Catherine was sure. There was a little girl outside.

And then she was gone.

Sarah? Was it Sarah?

A wave of excitement swept over Catherine, followed by a jolt of panic.

Am I seeing things now?

She watched Dale as he looked back into the yard. If he had seen her, he wasn't saying anything. And Catherine didn't want to ask him. Not until she was more certain about what she had or hadn't seen.

"You know, maybe I will go for a walk," she said, standing up. "Do a little exploring."

"Everything okay?" Dale asked.

Catherine sighed.

"Why does there always have to be a problem? Yes. Everything's fine. Stop worrying about me."

But as she turned to get dressed, Catherine tried to bury her own worry. Had she really seen someone? She needed to find out.

10

CATHERINE'S HEART hammered as she rushed into the backyard and followed the faint outline of a stone path that had all but vanished under the unkempt garden. She waded through the tall grass of the yard, feeling it brush against her legs. But there was no sign of any life at all, much less a young girl.

Catherine's mind swirled in uncertainty. Half-certain she had seen Sarah but also well aware that there was no way she could have. But, at the very least, there was a young girl. She was certain.

There's no way I imagined it, she thought. *It was too real.*

Noticing a narrow breach in the thicket, she decided to explore further. With a mix of dread and compulsion she slipped through the gap and into the thick woods behind it. A small trail led her deeper into the forest, where the dense canopy of pine, cypress and oak trees devoured the light and cast foreboding shadows all around her.

What the hell am I doing? This is insane.

Still, she felt compelled to press on. It was almost as if she didn't have a choice. She walked deeper into the woods, scouring the forest for any sign of the girl. Finally, she reached a fork in the path. Pausing to catch her breath, she wiped the cold sweat from her brow.

She heard a sudden rustle of leaves and spun around just in time to see the fleeting glimpse of yellow dashing behind a clump of trees.

"Hello?" she gently called out.

Edging closer, the figure seemed to dissolve into the dance of light and shadows, and Catherine laughed to herself for letting her imagination get the best of her.

Then, she heard the deliberate crunch of leaves behind her.

She turned just as a shadow slipped into the dense thicket.

"Who's there?" she yelled, her voice sharper and edged with fear.

She ventured off the path in the same direction that the shadowy figure had gone. She scanned the woods, looking for any movement. Her heart pounded as she turned in every direction.

A sense of panic began to well in her but, instead of running back, she found herself drawn toward it like a moth to a flame.

And then she heard something else.

A soft, eerie hum. A child's melody twisted by the wind and left floating in the trees. It was ethereal. Almost soothing. But it sent shivers down Catherine's spine.

Feeling more certain than ever that the girl was real, Catherine walked toward the sound, each step heavier than the last. But, for some reason, the further into the woods she went, the more she felt as if she was being watched.

The elusive melody led her on a twisted path. Her pulse raced as she plunged deeper into the thick woods. Filled with dread, she was too afraid to call out. Afraid it would scare the child. Every instinct told her to go back, yet she pressed on, driven by a need she couldn't understand.

Finally, the claustrophobic grip of the woods began to give way, and Catherine emerged from the woods to find a serene pond. Its still surface served as a perfect mirror to the cloudless, light blue sky above. Dragonflies flittered between the tall cattails that stood like silent sentinels along the pond's edge. Spanish moss hung gracefully from a lone cypress tree that emerged from the shallow waters. Catherine let out a sigh, basking in the welcome tranquility that quickly replaced the paranoia that had brought her here.

She noticed an old boathouse jutting out into the water about fifty yards ahead. And while it was so faint she couldn't be sure, the humming seemed to be coming from inside.

11

———

CATHERINE WALKED SLOWLY toward the boathouse, her curiosity battling a sense of dread. Like everything else on the property, the boathouse was in a state of neglect and disrepair. Time and the elements had peeled away most of the red paint, exposing the weathered gray wood underneath. Next to the boathouse, a decaying wooden pier had begun to sink into the water.

But Catherine didn't care about any of that. She was fixated on the haunting melody that seemed to come from inside the boathouse. It had to be the girl she had seen in the yard.

"Hello," she called out, not wanting to scare the child.

But no one answered and the humming continued.

Catherine slowly stepped closer to the boathouse. She noticed bubbles rising from a single spot in the pond not far from the boathouse. They sent a series of ripples across the still waters, echoing out in circles until they faded away.

And then the humming stopped.

Catherine froze in the silence, waiting for something to happen. She could feel her heart pounding in her temple. And then, the door to the boathouse began to creak open.

Catherine paused, waiting for the child to emerge. But the doorway remained empty.

"Hello," Catherine called out again, her voice quivering. "It's okay. I just wanted to say hi."

As if in response, the door slammed shut.

Catherine gasped. Her heart thundered and her breath quickened. Every instinct she had told her to run away, but she needed to know. As she slowly walked toward the boathouse, a foul stench assaulted her senses. She covered her mouth and nose, the repulsive air clawing at her throat, and soldiered on until she found herself standing directly in front of the door.

Her hand trembled as she reached out to grab the door handle. To her surprise, it was ice cold. She took a deep breath and hesitantly pushed the door open.

Just inside the door, a large black snake quickly slithered into the water. The sudden movement scared Catherine and she staggered back. At the same time, a cacophony of fluttering wings exploded as a flock of ducks shot into the sky. Frightened by the sudden chaos, Catherine toppled backwards to the ground.

She leaned forward, looking into the boathouse. It was hard to see into the shadowy interior. She stared into the darkness, looking for any sign of movement.

"Hello?" she asked.

Her timid question was answered by a rustle in the hydrangea bushes behind her. She turned to once again see a flash of yellow. Except now, in the open sun, she could clearly tell it was a person.

"Who's there?" she yelled. "I can see you."

A man slowly stood up, an angry scowl across his weathered, severe face.

"Have you been spying on me?" Catherine snapped.

The man timidly approached Catherine; his head hung in embarrassment. Even though it was already hot outside, Catherine couldn't help but notice he was wearing an LSU sweatshirt. Purple with splashes of yellow. She struggled to her feet but slipped in the wet grass and fell again to her knees.

The man extended a hand to her, but Catherine, uncomfortable with accepting his help, pulled herself up slowly on her own.

"Were you watching me?" Catherine asked.

"You're not supposed to be here," the man finally said in a thick Cajun accent.

He still avoided eye contact, and even though his words were benign, they had an anger to them that kept Catherine on edge.

"It's okay. I'm staying at Henry Devereux's house."

"Henry," Virgil said, shaking his head in what Catherine assumed was disapproval.

"I'm married to Dale, Henry's son."

"Dale," he said, nodding.

And then he looked her in the eyes for the first time. They were wide and filled with fear.

"Shouldn't be here," he said.

"I'm sorry. I heard a little girl singing," she said. "Did you see her?"

Before he could answer, they were both distracted by someone walking down a gravel path toward them. It was Dale.

"There you are," Dale said. "I see you've met Virgil. Hello, Virgil. Do you remember me?"

From the way he spoke to the old man, Catherine gathered that the old man must have a learning disability of some sort. He answered Dale with a slight nod.

"I see you've met my wife," Dale said, putting his arm around Catherine. "Cat, this is our neighbor, Virgil."

Dale pointed through the trees to a barely visible house.

"He lives through there. Man, Virgil. I haven't seen you in a long time. How are you? How's your mom?"

Virgil looked to the ground again.

"Mama passed on. It's just me now."

"Oh, I'm so sorry to hear that," Dale said.

"She should not be down here," Virgil said.

"I'm so sorry," Catherine said. "I got lost in the woods and–"

"Not by water," Virgil continued. "Bad things happen by water."

And then he turned and walked away.

Dale chuckled.

"Nice seeing you, Virgil!"

Dale turned toward Catherine.

"He's just a bit off, but harmless," Dale said. "He acts like this is his land, but it's ours. So don't mind him. What were you doing out here anyway?"

Catherine looked back at the empty boathouse, still confused. But she decided to keep it to herself for now.

"Just exploring," she said. "It's really pretty out here."

"Yeah. Well, we should get back before it gets unbearable. And to clean you up."

Catherine looked down at the mud on her clothes and grass stains on her hands and knees.

"What? I chose this look."

The two laughed as they headed back up the path. Unaware that, behind them, the boathouse door quietly swung shut.

12

LATER THAT NIGHT, Catherine lay in bed replaying the events of the day. She had kept her eyes peeled the rest of the day in hopes of seeing the girl again. Still, there was enough uncertainty that she decided not to tell Dale about her experience. She knew he was skeptical that she was actually doing better, and he had hinted more than once that he believed she should have stayed at the treatment center longer. She probably had just let her imagination get the best of her. While he didn't admit to it, she suspected Virgil was probably the one she had heard humming. Because of the lilting, innocent nature of the song, she had simply mistaken it as a child's voice. Still, regardless of whether it was real or not, the entire episode had been unsettling and left her nerves frayed.

She glanced at Dale, sleeping soundly on the other side of the bed. What she would give for a good night's sleep. Even on the rare occasions she managed to fall asleep, nightmares were guaranteed to interrupt her slumber. It had gotten to the point that she dreaded bedtime.

Her brain spinning with restless anxiety, she slipped out of bed and padded quietly into the hallway. The bathroom was next door and Catherine stepped inside, softly clicking the door shut before turning on the light. She splashed water on her face and patted it dry with a hand towel. Finding a small glass in the medicine cabinet, she filled it with water and reached for the bottle of sleeping pills she had brought with her.

As she began to twist the child-proof lid, she was distracted by the sound of dripping water. She looked at the faucet and checked the tub. It wasn't coming from the obvious places. She grew still, trying to identify the source.

When it was clear the sound wasn't coming from the bathroom, she stepped into the hallway and followed the steady, slow drip as it echoed in the darkness of the long corridor, guiding her to a door that was slightly ajar. Her senses buzzed and her breath quickened as she stood in front of it, peering into the sliver of darkness.

Maybe I should get Dale, she wondered. *What if there's a leak? What am I going to do?*

But before she could even process the thought, she found herself pushing the door open. She fumbled around on the wall for the light switch and flipped it, only to find it didn't work. She stood motionless in the doorway, staring into the empty darkness and listening to the persistent drip, as she waited for her eyes to adjust.

The room gradually revealed itself. Even though it was very dark, she could tell the room was unused. What little furniture there was had been draped in white sheets that had taken on a gray velvet sheen from the layers of dust. A few boxes littered the hardwood floor, and a child's rocking chair sat facing a corner. A deep musty odor permeated the air.

Catherine searched for the source of the drip. She checked the windows to see if one was possibly open and the sound was coming from outside. But they were all sealed shut. Then something shiny on the floor near the rocking chair caught her eye. She inched closer and saw a small puddle of water.

She looked to the ceiling for a leak but found nothing. In fact, there was no apparent source for the water.

Then the dripping stopped.

Catherine froze. A chill of dread washed over her. The sudden silence pressed in on her, and she became aware of her own breath. Then she heard something else – a strange noise. At first it sounded like swirling wind, but it soon became apparent it was a whispering voice. A child's whispering voice.

She knew she should fight the whispers. To take deep breaths and push them away. But she found herself straining to understand what they were saying. Finally, the words became clear:

"Help me, Mommy. Help me."

Catherine gasped. A bolt of terror shot through her, and she was too petrified to even scream.

This isn't happening. Not again. This isn't real, she thought as she covered her ears.

"No. No. No," she muttered, shaking her head and repeating the mantra she'd been taught to combat the voices that used to torment her. "You're not real. You're not real."

As suddenly as it started, the whispers stopped.

Catherine stood still in the deathly silence, her breath shallow. She glanced back at the rocker. The water puddle was gone.

A million thoughts flooded her brain.

What just happened? Was that Sarah? Why does she need my help? Did I just imagine all of this?

She felt herself beginning to hyperventilate and struggled to keep her composure. She took a deep breath and wiped her face of any possible tears.

It's not real, she repeated in her mind, not really believing it. *It's not real.*

But it began to calm her down, and as soon as she felt the panic begin to retreat, she left the room as quickly as she could. Pulling the door shut quietly, she turned, only to recoil in panic at the presence of someone standing in front of her.

It was Dale.

She breathed a sigh of relief.

"What the hell are you doing?" he asked with a half-smile.

Catherine put on her bravest face. *He mustn't know.*

"I thought I heard a noise," she said, trying to steady her trembling voice.

Dale opened the door and peeked inside.

"In here?" he asked. "Probably mice."

"Probably," she agreed, forcing a smile.

"Or maybe a ghost," he said with a mischievous grin.

Catherine didn't respond with the laugh he expected, and he noticed she was out of breath.

"Everything okay?" he asked.

Catherine kissed him on the cheek and took his hand, leading him back to their room.

"I'm just tired," she said.

13
———

CATHERINE DIDN'T SLEEP at all the rest of the night. Although, as part of nature's cruel joke, she finally dozed off around 6 a.m. She woke an hour later, the small taste of sleep only serving as a reminder of what she didn't have.

As she lay in bed, the memories of the previous night's horror lingered in her mind.

Was that Sarah? Was she trying to contact her? Was she in trouble?

Or was Catherine's own guilt driving her insane? It all seemed so real, but none of it made any sense. Maybe she had been sleepwalking. It had all been a dream and she had snapped out of it while standing in the middle of the room.

While she didn't really buy that story, she forced herself to accept it, and buried any other possibility with all the other instances she'd experienced since her daughter's death. She tried to remember how she had acted around Dale. And how he had responded. The last thing she wanted was to give him more reason to worry about her mental state. His need to get back to normal seemed to be so strong, she worried what he would do if she appeared too 'stuck' or fragile. Would he try to have her committed? Would he leave her?

As the jumble of thoughts spun around in her head like a rusty hamster wheel, she became aware of muffled voices reverberating through the vents of the old house. Catherine's curiosity got her out of bed. She shuffled into the hallway, glancing toward the shut door of the abandoned room before walking toward the stairs. Toward the voices.

As she got closer, the mumbles began to materialize into familiar voices. It was Dale and Henry. They were arguing. Catherine stayed out of view so she could listen.

"This house is big, but y'all still wake me up walking around in the middle of the night," Henry snapped.

"She just has trouble sleeping," Dale pleaded.

Catherine slid to the floor. Upset that she had made an enemy out of Henry, but relieved that Dale was still defending her.

In the parlor, the two men's argument continued.

"Why are you really here?" Henry asked. "And don't give me any of that crap about making sure I'm okay. You haven't checked on me since you kicked me out of your house."

Behind him, the Tiffany lamp flickered then turned off. Henry groaned and wheeled over, pulling the chain to turn it back on.

"That was unfortunate," Dale said. "But you have to

understand. You were supposed to be watching our daughter. She was a baby."

"I did not hurt her," Henry replied.

"When we came home, she was crawling on the floor in the kitchen, and you were passed out drunk in the living room. Thank God we got home when we did."

"Afraid she was gonna cook her own dinner?"

"Why do you always have to make a joke?" Dale asked.

"Why do you always have to be so serious?" Henry replied. "So, I drank too much. Everything turned out fine. You didn't have to kick me out. I never got a chance to see her..."

His voice trailed off and tears began to well up against his will.

"I didn't even get to say goodbye," he stammered.

Seeing his father fight back tears was something Dale wasn't accustomed to and it immediately disarmed him.

"I didn't either," he replied softly. "I'm sorry."

Henry nodded, fighting back his emotions and clenching his jaw to summon his inflated pride.

"Is that why you're really here?" he asked. "Running back to daddy because you're sad?"

Dale looked into his father's eyes, back to their familiar steely glare. He shook his head, tired of fighting.

"I'm here because you're my father," Dale said.

"Please. You think that fixes what you did? You kicked me out. And then you abandoned me. Just like everyone else."

"Abandoned you?" Dale argued, his voice rising. "You practically ran me out of this house when I was a kid."

Henry's face turned red with anger.

"You're going to put this on me?" he yelled. "After everything I've been through?"

"You went through?" Dale yelled back. "You? What about me? I was just a kid!"

"I needed time!"

"Well, I needed a father!"

Henry glared at his son. Then he spun his wheelchair around and rolled out of the room.

14

CATHERINE MANAGED to avoid both men for most of the morning, unable – or unwilling – to face their scorn. Even though she came along on this trip kicking and screaming, she also hoped that having Dale around his father would give them both a chance to mend their broken fences. And distract Dale enough so he wasn't so focused on her shortcomings.

But Dale was different around his father now. Maybe his passing out while watching Sarah was the last straw or maybe this deep-seated rage was how he dealt with his grief. But he managed to keep it buried most of the time. Leave it to Henry to be able to bring it to the surface. Either way, Catherine had never seen this angry side of Dale. And it scared her.

She finally sought refuge in the kitchen, where Delphine was cleaning the sink.

"I swear. That man must think this sink is magic," she complained. "You just put your dirty dishes in this magic bowl, and they somehow get cleaned and put away."

Catherine chuckled.

"Dale is the same way," she said. Her voice was tired and soft.

Delphine put the hand towel on the counter and pointed at the coffeemaker.

"I just made a fresh pot," she said. "Sounds like you could use some."

Catherine smiled and pulled a mug from the cupboard.

"You want any?" she asked as she filled her cup.

"I've already had my daily dose," Delphine said. "Anymore, I'll be cleaning the ceilings. And I don't get paid for that."

The women sat across from each other at the long wooden kitchen table.

"I hear you had a bit of a night," Delphine said.

Catherine looked up over her coffee cup.

Dale must have shared more than I thought.

Not wanting to talk about it, she changed the subject.

"Do any children live around here?" Catherine asked.

The question startled Delphine.

"Children?" Delphine asked, shaking her head. "Not that I know of. Why do you ask?"

Catherine shook her head.

"Nothing," she said. "I just thought I saw a little girl in the yard yesterday."

Delphine nodded knowingly.

"Where?"

"Along the back hedges," Catherine answered. "She must have just wandered in accidentally."

"Hmmm," Delphine replied. "No children around

here that I know of. But even if there were, the only house anywhere near here is the Trahan's old home way back beyond the pond."

"Is that where Virgil lives?"

Delphine nodded.

"Virgil Trahan," she replied. "He's a simple man. Lives there all by his lonesome since his mama died. He may act a little rough around the edges, but he's harmless."

"I met him yesterday," Catherine said. "He is a bit of an odd duck."

"Ain't we all," Delphine replied with a smile.

Catherine nodded.

"About this girl," Delphine said. "What'd she look like?"

"I didn't get a good look, honestly," Catherine replied. "Maybe it was just the sun playing tricks on my eyes."

"Don't dismiss what you can't explain," Delphine said, standing up from the table. "Sometimes the world shows you what you need to see."

Catherine considered telling her about the episode in the empty room. Delphine could tell something was on her mind.

"What is it, child?" she asked gently. "Come on. Spit it out."

Catherine decided against saying anything and shook her head. She didn't need the one friend she had thinking she was crazy.

15

CATHERINE WAS INTRIGUED by what Delphine had said about the world showing you what you need to see, and almost told her about the voices she had heard the night before but decided better of it. She was still convinced it was all in her head and it was best not to let anyone else in. It was all just the stress of being in a strange place. She just needed to relax.

That afternoon, Dale drove Henry into town for a doctor's appointment and Delphine went along to help. Dale had invited Catherine to come with them, but she was more excited to have a little bit of alone time. She could tell that Dale was concerned about leaving her alone, but she convinced him she'd be fine.

"It's actually exactly what I need," she had told him.

Promising to be back in an hour or two, the three left and Catherine breathed a sigh of relief.

Alone at last, she thought.

She decided to take a long bath to refresh her mind and body. Heading upstairs, she looked down the hallway toward the door of the abandoned room. She was tempted to explore it further but fought the temptation. She found herself repeating what Dale had told her.

You can't keep feeding the grief.

She went into the bathroom to prepare her bath. As the water filled the cast iron clawfoot tub, she found a towel in the linen closet. It was slightly musty from lack of use, but it would have to do. She spread it out and hung it over the bathroom sink so that it could air out as she bathed, hoping that would freshen it up a bit. Then, after passing her hand through the running water to check the temperature, she slid out of her clothes.

As soon as she sank into the tub, a sense of calm literally washed over her. Because it was an old tub, it was smaller. But, if Catherine bent her knees, she could slide down enough so her shoulders were under water. Closing her eyes, she could practically feel the hot water melting her stress away. Birds chirped out the window, complimenting the gentle splashes of the water as she moved her hands over the surface. Catherine smiled. This was better than any doctor visit.

She was so lost in her tranquil world that she barely noticed the birds had stopped chirping. When she finally became aware of the eerie silence, she opened her eyes. In the same moment, something unseen yanked her under water.

Instead of just hitting the bottom of the tub, Catherine was pulled deeper and deeper into dark waters. She struggled to find her way to the surface, but something kept pulling her further down until she was overcome with a sense of calm. She stopped struggling and relaxed, floating serenely in the abyss. And even though she was underwater, breathing wasn't a concern.

The water was so dark, she could barely see her hand in front of her face. But she became aware of another presence. Looking to the right, she sensed a mass floating toward her. As it got closer, she could see it was a body. A young girl. As the calmness fled her body, Catherine's heart began to pound. Other than long, blonde hair, it was too dark to make out any details, but she could tell the body was facing away from her. And then it turned toward her. Its face decomposed beyond recognition. Its dead, lifeless eyes staring directly into Catherine's.

Catherine began to thrash in the water, trying to get away from the grotesque corpse. She struggled to make her way to the surface, leaving the body below her, but just as she was about to break the surface, a hand seemed to hold her down.

Catherine fought against the hand with all her strength, but it continued to hold her under. It slid down and wrapped its long fingers around her throat, gripping tightly. As she tried to wrestle free of its grasp, the arm turned into a black snake and coiled around her neck, squeezing.

Catherine opened her eyes, gasping for air. She was sitting up in the tub. Her hair wasn't even wet.

It couldn't have been a dream, she thought. *It felt real.*

Completely exhausted, she pulled herself out and over the edge the tub and collapsed on the floor, sobbing.

16

When Dale, Henry and Delphine returned, Catherine met them at the door with a forced smile and brave face. Dale was too preoccupied getting Henry out of the car and into his wheelchair to notice, but Delphine knew something was wrong right away. She stepped in the house and pulled Catherine in with her.

"Girl, what happened?" she asked.

"I'm fine," Catherine said.

Delphine looked at her with knowing eyes.

"If you say so. I ain't the prying type. Not my nature," she said with a smirk.

She walked away, talking back to Catherine as she went.

"If you need me, I'll be in the kitchen."

Catherine turned to see Dale struggling to push Henry up the makeshift ramp to the door.

"This ramp is working great," Henry said sarcastically.

"It's temporary," Dale growled. "And you can help, you know. That thing is motorized."

"Oh, it is," Henry said, mocking surprise. "I forgot all about that."

He winked at Catherine as he pressed the button and drove up the ramp, leaving a worn-out Dale behind. Dale gave Catherine a peck on the cheek as he walked past her.

"I may have to kill him," he said quietly.

"Glad to see you two getting along," Catherine teased, pretending to laugh.

She shut the door behind the two men, who continued to bicker as they moved into the house. She relaxed, the fake smile falling from her face. Even though she had tried to shake it, she was obviously still shell-shocked from the earlier incident in the tub and decided to take Delphine up on her offer.

Catherine walked into the kitchen, where Delphine was sipping a cup of coffee.

"Why I thought it would be a good idea to venture out with those two is a mystery," Delphine said. "I've never heard such non-stop squabbling. They're worse than an old married couple."

Catherine leaned back against the counter. She didn't even bother to fake a smile.

"You want to talk about it?" Delphine said.

"I think I'm losing my mind," Catherine blurted out.

Delphine studied her, deciding how much to share. Finally, she shook her head.

"No, child. You're perfectly sane," she said. "It's this house."

Delphine took a long sip from her coffee cup and stood.

"Why don't we go for a little walk?" She asked. "It's beautiful outside and I think you could use some fresh air."

She walked to the back door in the kitchen and opened it, looking back at a still-stunned Catherine.

"You coming?"

17

Delphine led Catherine to the trail that led into the woods.

"We'll get a little more privacy out here," she explained. "Mr. Henry's favorite hobby is eavesdropping."

They casually strolled in silence for a while until Delphine finally spoke.

"So, what happened?"

Catherine hesitated, almost afraid to say the words.

"You'll think I'm crazy," she finally said.

"Honey, I don't believe in crazy," Delphine answered. "Now go on. Talk to me."

Catherine took a deep breath and then told Delphine about the incident in the tub.

"It seemed more real than any dream I've ever had."

Delphine nodded as she listened.

"But I'm guessing it wasn't the first time something like that happened. Am I right?" she asked.

Catherine nodded. "The night before, I went into that empty room upstairs, down the hall from Dale's. I thought I heard water dripping. And then I heard a little girl whispering. Clear as day."

"Was it your daughter?" Delphine asked.

"It would have to be, right?"

"What did she say?"

Tears began to roll down Catherine's face.

"She said 'Help me, Mommy.'"

The words caught in Catherine's throat, but she quickly suppressed her emotions and even pretended to laugh as she wiped the tears from her eyes.

"I told you," she said. "I'm losing my mind."

"You poor child," Delphine said, slipping her arm into Catherine's and patting it. "May I ask you a personal question?"

Catherine smiled, but Delphine sensed her discomfort.

"I think we've already crossed that bridge," Catherine said.

"I don't think you're losing your mind," Delphine said. "I think you're opening it."

Delphine turned over Catherine's arm so they both could see the scar on her wrist.

"How far did you go?" Delphine asked. "When this happened?"

Catherine pulled her arm away. Then Delphine pulled up her sleeve, showing Catherine an old ashen scar along her own wrist.

"I'm sorry," Catherine said. "I had no idea."

"Long time ago," Delphine said. "I thought I was losing my mind, too. All the voices."

"You heard voices?" Catherine asked.

"When you tried to take your life, did you get close?" Delphine asked, ignoring Catherine's question. "To the other side?"

Catherine crossed her arms in front of her, thinking about a moment she'd trained herself to forget.

"Dale told me the doctors said my heart had stopped for two minutes before they revived me."

"Did you see anything?" Delphine asked. "A light? A glow? A feeling?"

Catherine shook her head.

"I don't remember anything," she replied.

"Sometimes our mind protects us from what we know," Delphine said. "But sometimes, something slips through anyway. If you were gone for a couple of minutes, maybe... maybe you opened a door."

Catherine laughed.

"Oh, I'm sure Dale would love it if I told him that theory."

"Dale don't understand, so Dale don't need to know," Delphine said curtly, before returning to her calmer tone. "But I know this. Some people are born with it, and some get it when they cross over before their time. Maybe that's what happened to you."

"I don't even know what that means," Catherine said.

"Do you think your daughter is trying to contact you?" Delphine asked.

"Do you?" Catherine asked, tears welling up in her eyes.

"Only you can know that," Delphine said.

Catherine suddenly found it hard to breathe. "There's more," she said.

Catherine then told Delphine everything. About the humming in the woods, the nightmare of the car in the water. She stopped and turned to Delphine.

"I feel like she's terrorizing me," Catherine said. "Does she hate me? Does she blame me? Oh God. She does. She hates me."

Catherine began to cry, and Delphine pulled her into her arms.

"You don't know that," Delphine said. "Sometimes spirits have to poke at strong emotions to connect and fear is the easiest. Sometimes they just get frustrated they can't communicate with us. So, they lash out."

She took Catherine's hands into her own and looked her in the eyes.

"The truth is, I don't know," Delphine said. "But, Sweetheart, I do know this: If she came to you, it's for a reason. And you'd be a damned fool not to find out what it is."

She squeezed Catherine's hands, letting it sink in. Catherine finally nodded.

"How?" she finally asked.

"You just gotta be open to it," Delphine said. "And you gotta be open to any possibility."

She noticed the concerned look on Catherine's face and responded to it with a warm smile.

"Don't worry, child," she said, patting Catherine's arm. "I'll help you."

"What do I tell Dale?" Catherine asked.

"It's probably best you don't tell him a thing," Delphine replied.

18

It took a while for her to build up the nerve, but Catherine gathered the courage to return to the empty room. After making sure no one else was around, she walked slowly down the corridor and stood in front of the foreboding door.

Am I being stupid? Am I just indulging my own overactive imagination?

But what Delphine had told her only confirmed what she had feared. And her new friend was right. She needed to find out what Sarah wanted. She also needed to tell her daughter how sorry she was. She had even allowed herself to entertain thoughts of reconciling with her daughter's spirit, allowing her to spend more time with the child that was taken from her too soon.

She sucked in a deep inhale and reached out to the doorknob.

"Catherine?" she heard Dale's voice coming up the stairs and she snatched her hand back, turning to face him just as he reached the top of the stairs.

"There you are," he said with a smile. "What are you doing?"

She walked back toward him, forcing a casual grin.

"Looking for you," she replied.

"Yeah, sorry," he said. "I was outside, hauling the wood around front to build the ramp. I wondered if you'd want to help me. There's a decent breeze and it's starting to cool off."

"An afternoon of manual labor in the Louisiana sun," Catherine teased, kissing Dale on the cheek. "You really know how to show a girl a good time."

"I just figure some activity could do us both good," Dale said. "And the sooner we get the ramp built, the sooner we can leave."

"I'll be out in a minute, okay?"

Dale nodded and she watched him walk back down the stairs. As soon as she heard the front door shut, she returned to the room. The interruption put a sense of urgency to her experiment, and this time, she opened the door without hesitation.

It was far less menacing by the light of day. And much dustier. She walked around the room, truly not knowing what she was looking for.

"Sarah?" she asked out loud. "Are you here, baby?"

The silent response was deafening.

"Sarah. Mommy's here. I'm so sorry, baby. I'm so, so sorry."

Her heart grew heavier as she spoke and she walked to the window, intending to open it and let in some fresh air. The window overlooked what used to be the garden in the backyard. From this vantage point, Catherine could make out more of the sculptures and hedge work that were buried at eye level.

And then Catherine saw her.

A young girl stood at the back of the yard, facing her direction. She had blonde hair and wore the same yellow dress as before and, even though her face was hidden in the shadows, she seemed to be staring up at Catherine.

Catherine took a step back. A swirl of emotions filled her. Shock. Horror. Excitement. Nervousness. And relief.

"You heard me," Catherine said.

19

CATHERINE COULD HEAR the metallic scream of a circular saw as Dale worked in the front of the house. But instead of going to help him, Catherine walked out the back door.

She beelined it to the back of the yard, her eyes trained on the area where she had seen the little girl. Suddenly aware that Henry may be watching her, she ducked behind some bushes, out of view from the house. The area toward the back of the estate seemed empty, and Catherine worried that she had lost her opportunity.

"Sarah?" she called out. "Mommy's here, baby."

Catherine walked along the overgrown thickets that lined the rear of the yard.

"Sarah?"

She stopped and listened. Hoping maybe she would hear her daughter talking again. Or even hear her humming. But all she heard was the loud jeering of a blue jay.

Her heart sank and she started to retreat to the house.

But something seemed to pull her toward the woods. Unsure if it was a hunch or just a compulsion, she pushed herself through the opening in the hedges, scratching her arm against the overgrown branches.

She became lost in her pursuit, suddenly oblivious to how strange her behavior seemed. Her entire body buzzed with a mix of excitement and fear as she walked toward the unknown, not even sure what she was hoping to find.

She trudged down the path, stopping every so often to call out to her daughter and listen for any type of response. But there was nothing. The air was still and thick with humidity. Catherine wiped the sweat from her forehead as she forged on, this time staying on the dirt path as it meandered through the woods.

It was only a couple of minutes before the trail brought her back to the pond. The sun was lower in the sky this time, draping the pond in the shadow of the tall cypress tree. No longer in the bright sun, the boat house appeared even more ominous, but Catherine was still inexplicably drawn to it.

"Sarah?" she called out again.

Even though she was expecting it, the repulsive odor still assaulted her senses and Catherine's eyes began to tear up as she walked closer and closer to the boathouse. She reached for the door handle and shook it loudly, hoping to scare off any waiting reptiles. And then she pushed the door open.

The interior seemed even darker than last time. The dank odor was almost overwhelming. But Catherine still stepped inside.

"Sarah?" she called out quietly, her voice shaking.

She looked around but didn't see anything of interest. The wide platform in front of her extended the length of the boathouse, opening on the right to a rowboat floating in the still water of the dock. On the wall to her left, several hooks held a few coils of old rope, some fishing gear and a spare set of oars.

She squinted into the darkness, toward the wall straight ahead of her. Something in the blackness seemed to move.

Is that a person? she wondered.

Slowly, she began to make out what appeared to be the shape of a child. The dark shape didn't move. It could all just be in her imagination. But Catherine felt certain it was real.

"Sarah," she said gently. "Is that you, baby?"

And then the shadow disappeared.

Catherine looked around frantically.

"No. No. Sarah. Come back, baby. It's Mommy."

She began to cry, worried that Sarah was afraid of her.

"Mommy won't hurt you, baby," Catherine said. "I'm so sorry. I didn't mean for it to happen. I would never hurt you on purpose. Never."

And then, the shadow suddenly reappeared.

This time it seemed more ominous, and Catherine took a tentative step backwards.

"Sarah," she said meekly.

But the shadow began to grow and morph into something dark and menacing.

And then it rushed directly at Catherine.

Catherine screamed as she fell back out of the

doorway, hitting the ground hard. When she sat up, the shadow was gone.

Why is she trying to hurt me? she thought as she began to cry.

But she knew why. Sarah blamed her, and rightfully so.

"I'm so sorry," Catherine sobbed, rocking back and forth. "Mommy is so sorry."

Dale was walking on the path toward the pond when Catherine emerged from the woods.

"Where'd you run off to?" he asked. "What are you doing out here again?"

"I saw a deer," Catherine lied. "I didn't think there were any around here."

"And you chased it through the woods?" Dale asked with a laugh.

Catherine shrugged and pretended to laugh back, but as she got closer, Dale could see something was wrong.

"Babe, what's going on?" he asked. "Are you okay?"

"I'm fine," she said. "I think the humidity is getting to me."

Dale put his hand on her forehead.

"Jeez, you're freezing," he said.

Then he stopped her, looking her straight in the eyes.

"Are you sure everything is okay?" he asked.

Before she could answer, Dale was distracted by someone coming up behind her. She turned to see Virgil, still in his LSU sweatshirt.

"She can't be by the water!" Virgil yelled, frustrated.

"Virgil! Just the man I was looking for! Would you be interested in helping me build a handicap ramp for Henry? I'll pay you."

He smiled at Catherine.

"Hope you don't mind. I could tell you weren't that interested."

Catherine smiled back, relieved for the distraction but somewhat guilty that she had maybe let Dale down.

"I'll meet you back at the house," he said.

Catherine nodded and started walking back alone.

As the path emptied out next to the house, she saw Henry waiting for her in the open back doorway.

"Where's Dale?" he asked. "Y'all have a visitor."

20

CATHERINE FOLLOWED Henry into the formal living room, a massive room just off the main foyer. From the dated furniture and yellow and gold wallpaper, it was apparent the room had not been decorated since the seventies. A large bay window filled an entire wall of the room, although, like the rest of the house, the white plantation shutters were pulled shut. Fortunately, the room was still brightened by the large chandelier that hung from the domed ceiling.

A tall, slender man in his late 60s had been studying some of the photos that adorned the wall, but immediately turned his attention to Catherine as she walked into the room.

"Catherine Devereux," he said with a smile. "I've heard so much about you. And where is that husband of yours?"

"He's not far behind me," Catherine replied. "I'm sorry. You are..."

"Oh, forgive me. I'm Frank Mason," he said, shaking Catherine's hand. "So nice to finally meet you, my dear. I apologize for arriving unannounced, but when I heard I missed Dale at the clinic today, I rushed over as soon as I could."

Catherine smiled. Even though he had a formal appearance, he exuded a friendly warmth that immediately made her feel at ease. Henry, on the other hand, seemed less than impressed. He wheeled back to an end table where he had set his glass of bourbon.

"I should be the one apologizing," she replied. "I'm sorry for my appearance. I clearly wasn't expecting guests."

"I'll try not to take offense that I don't warrant a little makeup," Henry chided a smile.

Clearly, their visitor had lifted Henry's spirits as well.

"Doc has been bothering us all since the beginning of time," Henry replied. Catherine couldn't tell if he was teasing or not.

"It sometimes feels like it," Mason said. "I hope he's not milking this wheelchair thing too much."

"Henry?" Catherine mocked surprise. "Never."

"Oh. My. Lord," Dale exclaimed from the other side of the room. "Doc!"

A giant smile spread across Mason's face.

"Dale Devereux," Mason said.

The two men embraced warmly.

"How long has it been?" Dale asked.

"Too many years," Mason replied.

Dale motioned to Catherine.

"Cat, this is Doc. I mean Dr. Mason," Dale said. "I've told you about him."

"Yes, we just met," Catherine replied. "I was apologizing for my appearance. Dale here was trying to recruit me to help build Henry's ramp."

"Dale, that is not work for a lady," Mason said, then turning quickly to Catherine. "Not that you aren't capable, mind you. I'm sorry. I'm a product of my past. What used to be a compliment is sometimes seen as something else these days."

Dale, still beaming, put his arm around Mason.

"I can't believe it's really you," he said, turning to Catherine. "Do you know this was the first face I allegedly saw when I came into the world. At least that's what he tells me."

Henry slammed his glass down on the end table in a protest that no one seemed to notice.

"It's a small community," Mason said. "There are many people Dale's age that can make the same disturbing claim."

He pulled away from Dale and looked him up and down.

"It is good to see you. It's been too long. You both have been in my thoughts."

He held out a hand for Catherine, and she realized he knew everything about the death of Sarah and probably her subsequent struggles.

"I wish we were meeting under better circumstances," he said to Catherine, confirming her suspicions. "I'm terribly sorry for your loss."

Catherine nodded politely. She felt exposed and ashamed.

"I know it's cliché," he continued. "But if there is anything I can do, please let me know."

"So, Henry tells me that you've practically retired," Dale interjected, sensing Catherine's discomfort, especially after their earlier conversation.

"I tried, honestly," he said. "But the town has grown, and more people mean more patients. I hired a staff, as you saw today, but I can't just walk away from it."

"Can't or won't?" Henry asked, finally chiming in.

Mason smiled.

"I do miss the days when we were a small town, and things were simpler. Now doctor visits have been replaced by Zoom calls or what not. I haven't kept up nor do I have any intention to do so."

"I wish more doctors would put quality before efficiency," Catherine replied.

"I'm afraid you are in the ever-shrinking minority," Mason replied with a chuckle.

"So, is there a Mrs. Mason?" Catherine asked.

Henry laughed out loud, but Mason ignored him.

"I'm afraid not," he said. "It just was never meant to be."

"Saved you from a world of heartache," Henry said.

Mason smiled politely. "Quite possibly."

Catherine watched her husband as he spoke to Dr. Mason. He was smiling and laughing. It was the lighthearted side of Dale she had almost forgotten about. She felt guilty, knowing he was afraid or even ashamed to show this side to her anymore. And he was probably right. Ever since Sarah's death, she was so lost in her own grief that she bristled at his attempts at lifting her out of it. But she was also resentful that he didn't seem to feel the pain like she did. Did he resent her as well? Was her pain driving him away? Maybe he really wanted to have her put into a treatment facility. Make her someone else's problem so he could enjoy life again.

She was pulled out of her paranoid thoughts when Delphine walked into the room. She seemed stunned by Mason's presence.

"I'm sorry," she said. "I didn't realize you had company. Does anyone need anything?"

Henry shook his glass, so the ice clanged loudly.

"I need another drink," he announced. "Anybody else?"

"Stay for dinner, Doc," Dale said.

"I'm afraid he was just leaving," Henry said, glaring up at the doctor.

Mason took the hint gracefully.

"Your father's right. Thank you for the kind offer, but I'm afraid I can't," Mason replied with a slight bow. "I have many more house calls on my list. But I just had to stop by and see how the prodigal son is doing."

The two men hugged again.

"It is so good to see you," Dale said.

"We'll get together soon to really catch up," Mason said. He turned to Catherine and kissed her hand. "And such a pleasure to finally meet you. Don't let this man bully you into any more tedious labor. There are carpenters for that sort of thing."

"I will definitely do that," Catherine replied politely.

Dr. Mason patted Henry on the shoulder as he passed him.

"And for God's sake," Mason said with a wink. "Someone get this poor man a drink."

Dale walked Mason to the door as Catherine and Henry watched.

"Asshole," Henry grumbled under his breath.

21

LATE THAT NIGHT, Catherine and Dale lay in bed, about as far apart as possible. Dale faced away, trying hard to fall asleep, but Catherine stared up at the ceiling, lost in thought.

She tried to make sense of what happened earlier at the boathouse.

Who was this girl?

She seemed so real, but Delphine had assured her there were no children in the area. It had to be Sarah. She had blonde hair like Sarah. She looked to be the same age as Sarah. But it couldn't be Sarah. She was...

She could write off the thing in the boathouse as her eyes playing tricks on her. Just shadows mixing with her own imagination. But she was certain she had seen the girl. And, as hard as it was to accept, it had to be Sarah's ghost.

She wanted to talk to Dale about it, but she knew better than to tell him she was seeing their dead daughter. He'd think she'd lost it for sure. Delphine had told her to be open to it, but open to what? What did Sarah want from her? What was she supposed to do?

Catherine not only felt confused and frustrated, she also felt very, very alone. She tried to think about something else. Dr. Mason seemed like a nice man. Dale had mentioned him before, and she couldn't shake how much Dale lit up when he saw the older man. She also couldn't help but notice that Henry didn't share that same enthusiasm. Her father-in-law was always a curmudgeon, but he seemed extra spiteful with Dr. Mason, and she couldn't help but sense some bad blood.

It was not only the perfect distraction for her overactive mind, but it was something she could safely talk to Dale about.

"You awake?" she finally asked.

"If I answered no, would you believe me?" Dale mumbled. "Can't sleep again?"

"What's the deal with your father and Dr. Mason?"

Dale laughed and turned to face her.

"The deal?" he asked, his eyes still shut.

"Please tell me you know what I'm talking about."

Dale smiled and finally opened his eyes to look at his wife.

"Henry's just proud," he said. "He was never there for me growing up. But Doc was. He knew Henry had his demons and I'm sure he saw how neglected I was, so he filled in the gap. Got me out of the house. Took me to county fairs. Ball games. That kind of stuff. So, I naturally became closer to him. And Henry resented him for it."

"Seems kind of childish," Catherine replied.

"Henry? Childish? Nahh."

Dale kissed Catherine on the cheek.

"Get some sleep," he said. "Take a pill if you have to."

He rolled over again, but Catherine, still feeling the pangs of loneliness, scooted closer to him and put her arm around him. It was something she hadn't done in a very long time. Dale couldn't help but smile and was gently snoring in minutes.

An hour later, Catherine was still awake. She rolled away from Dale and quietly slid out of bed. She tiptoed out of the bedroom and stared down toward the door of the abandoned room. Her curiosity pulled her toward it, but her exhaustion kept her at bay. She had endured enough unsettling encounters for one day.

She crept downstairs and into the kitchen to get a glass of water. She didn't want to risk waking anyone, so she fumbled in the dark, opening a cabinet to find a plastic tumbler and feeling her way to the sink where she filled it with water.

"Can't sleep?"

Henry's voice scared her to death. She dropped the cup in the sink and spun around to see her father-in-law sitting in the shadows behind her.

"Jesus, Henry."

"Someone's jumpy," he said.

He rolled over with an empty glass, obviously drunk, and opened a bottom cabinet to pull out a full bottle of bourbon.

"I haven't had a good night's sleep in thirty years," he

said as he set the glass on the table and opened the bottle. "I hate the night. So damn quiet."

He poured himself a drink then offered the bottle to Catherine. She shook her head no. Henry shrugged and pushed the stopper back down into the bottle.

"Suit yourself. There's cookies in the cabinet."

Catherine grabbed her cup from the sink and refilled it with water.

"I just wanted some water. I'm going back to bed now."

Henry sighed.

"Hold on."

She begrudgingly turned to face him.

"I know you took a big hit," he said. "And I know it hurts like hell."

"But I need to just get over it," Catherine interrupted. "I know."

But Henry shook his head.

"That's bullshit," he said. "Everyone will tell you things like 'time heals all wounds.' But it's a crock of shit. Time only makes it worse."

Catherine was stunned by the words. It was the first time someone spoke candidly to her since her daughter died.

"The night this happened," he continued, patting the wheelchair. "I was pissing and moaning, three sheets to the wind. I even thought I saw a ghost. Scared the shit out of me. I backed up and fell down the stairs."

He took a long drink of his bourbon. Catherine wanted to ask about the ghost but thought better of it.

"That was just a few months ago. I'd been whining

and bitching and cursing God for so long, He just got sick of it and pushed me right down my own stairs. Gave me something to really cry about."

He laughed to himself, then looked up at Catherine. It was dark, but she was sure he had tears in his eyes.

"And you know what? Didn't help. I still miss her every single damn day."

He drank the rest of the bourbon in his glass.

"That pain you're feeling? You won't get over it. You can't get over it. Best you can do is learn to fake it good enough that everyone'll think you're okay."

He laughed to himself.

"I never got that last part down. But the point is, even if you fool everyone else, when the lights go out and it gets quiet, you know."

"Did you forgive him?" Catherine asked. "For pushing you down the stairs?"

"God?" Henry asked. "Hell, no."

He grabbed the bottle and began to roll back to his bedroom. But he stopped in the kitchen doorway and turned around.

"Goodnight, Catherine," he said.

His voice was uncharacteristically gentle, and Catherine thought she detected a slight smile in the darkness. She nodded and smiled back, then Henry turned and rolled out of sight.

22

CATHERINE DRANK her glass of water and then headed back to bed, mulling over the conversation with Henry. Was he trying to give her advice or was he tormenting her? Knowing how he seemingly regarded her, it was hard to give him the benefit of the doubt. Yet he did seem sincere.

Starting up the stairs, she noticed one of the photos was askew. The same one that had been off kilter when she first arrived. But this time, as she tried to straighten it, it practically jumped off the wall. It hit the wooden step with a crash and the glass shattered.

Catherine knelt to clean it up. Luckily, most of the glass stayed within the black frame. She picked up the few large fragments she could see in the dark and carried the broken glass and frame into the kitchen in search of a broom.

Turning a counter lamp on so she could see better, she tilted the photo over the trash can and carefully removed the photo from the shards of glass. It was a picture of a group of people enjoying a picnic, but upon closer inspection she noticed an almost unrecognizable younger Henry standing off to the side. He was holding a baby that Catherine naturally assumed was Dale. They were right on the edge of the photo and Catherine could tell a part of the picture had been cut off. She had to assume Henry had trimmed the full photograph to cut out his ex-wife. Dale's mother. She remembered Dale telling her how Henry had removed any memory of her. Photographs and keepsakes. And Dale was never allowed to ask about her.

How selfish do you have to be to forbid your own son from asking about his mother? she wondered.

As she studied the image, she heard something upstairs. It sounded like the pitter-patter of a child running.

Catherine climbed the stairs in search of the noise, still clutching the photo. Her heart raced as she peered down the long, dark hallway, looking for any movement, but praying to God she wouldn't see anything.

She crept down the hall, her eyes barely adjusting to the suffocating heavy blackness that quickly swallowed her. Something shimmered on the floor and, as she cautiously stepped forward, she realized it was a growing puddle of water seeping out from underneath the door.

She grew nervous. The normal instinct would be to walk away. To avoid the dread that lay in front of her. But something pulled her forward. Her breath caught in her throat as she got closer to the door, and she froze as she heard what sounded like small feet splashing on the other side. Once again, she found herself facing the door, uncertain whether to open it or not.

She shuddered as her feet felt the icy puddle of water. Her instincts told her to go back, to find Dale. To do anything other than what she found herself compelled to do: reach for the doorknob.

She didn't need to turn it. The moment her hand touched the cold brass knob, the door creaked open. The room beyond was dark but she could see water pouring in from an open window like an overflowing bathtub. Catherine stepped inside, her feet splashing with every step.

"Sarah?" she called out, her voice barely a whisper. "Are you in here?"

There was no response. Nothing but the lapping of water against her ankles. Catherine walked to the window and shut it, stopping the endless deluge of water. For a brief moment, a peaceful silence settled over the room, and a moment of clarity fell over her.

What am I doing?

She felt a drop of cold water splash on her forehead. Then another.

She looked up and horror gripped her as she saw the ceiling rippling and moving, as if it were water itself. In fact, she felt as if she was underwater, staring up at the undulating surface.

What is happening?

More water droplets began to swell and fall to the floor. Sensing movement to her right, she turned to see a dark stain spreading across a wall. It grew larger, water trickling, then streaming out of the expanding black void.

The wallpaper began to bubble and peel away, revealing a dark, crumbling wall. Catherine stepped back in terror, watching in dread as words began to form in the chaos.

HELP ME MOMMY

Catherine's eyes widened in sheer panic. She tried to scream, but no sound escaped. She stumbled backwards, falling into the growing pool of water on the floor. As she scrambled to her knees, everything instantly changed.

The floor was bone dry. She put her hands to her hair, it was also dry. The room was as she had seen it before - dusty and in disrepair. But not wet. The wall was also dry. There was no ripped wallpaper. And no words.

Bewildered and shaking, she stood and touched the wall to be sure. A wave of bone cold chills ran through her body, and she jerked her hand back. Then the wall began to move again.

A child's face pressed against the wallpaper from the other side, stretching it into a grotesque mask.

Catherine stumbled back, paralyzed by the aberration staring at her. Then she heard a child's whisper.

"Help me, mommy."

"Sarah..." the words barely eeked out of Catherine's mouth.

Still behind the mask of the wallpaper, the aberration became clearer, and Catherine could make out the face perfectly.

She was slammed with a whirlwind of emotions. Shock. Confusion. Anger. Sadness. Horror.

It wasn't Sarah.

Catherine's breath caught in her throat.

"You're.... not... my Sarah," Catherine gasped.

The child's face twisted into a monstrous image, violently lunging forward with a rage-filled scream.

Catherine fell to the floor, shielding herself in terror. And the room grew still.

Catherine slowly looked up. Once again, the wall had returned to normal. Tears streamed down her face, and she collapsed in despair, sobbing uncontrollably.

"You're not Sarah," she cried. "You're not Sarah."

She crumpled on the floor, repeating the words over and over.

23

———

DELPHINE POURED A STILL-TREMBLING Catherine another cup of coffee. Catherine nodded in appreciation, still lost in her terrifying memory of what just happened. She looked awful. Her eyes were red and puffy and dark circles had begun around them from lack of sleep.

"I'm sorry to bother you, but Dale wouldn't understand," she said, her voice weak and quivering.

"You did the right thing," Delphine said. "I was up anyway."

Delphine sat across the kitchen table from Catherine.

"You want to talk about it?"

Catherine took a long sip of coffee, the cup shaking in her trembling hands.

"You know what I remember most about my Sarah?" she asked. "Her laugh. God, I loved her laugh. It was from the gut, you know? You couldn't help but smile when you heard it."

Her mind shifted to a more sobering memory and Catherine took a deep breath before continuing.

"That last night, I had to work late, and Dale was out of town, so my friend Helen picked up Sarah from daycare. By the time I picked her up, she was already asleep, and I got her all the way to the car before she woke up. While I was buckling her in, I heard her precious little voice say, 'I love you, Mommy.'"

Catherine began to cry, and Delphine reached out to hold her hand.

"We sang songs for a bit and then she told me a stupid joke she made up. I don't even remember. But I do remember her laugh. I remember looking back at her in the rearview mirror and being filled with so much love. And then we drove on in silence.

"I don't even remember nodding off. I just remember waking up in the hospital. They told me I had swerved into the other lane. They actually tried to console me by saying it happened fast and she didn't feel any pain. Like I had somehow done her a favor."

Catherine looked up at Delphine with a sadness and vulnerability that broke Delphine's heart.

"A mother is supposed to protect her child," Catherine said.

She tried to collect herself and wiped the sloppy tears from her cheeks.

"I never got to tell her I'm sorry. I never got to say goodbye. And then I think I see her. She might be reaching out to me. Even if it was lashing out, it would give me a chance to talk to her again. Tell her I love her so much. And maybe, just maybe, to hear her laugh again."

Delphine gave Catherine room to grieve, but finally broke the silence.

"Maybe this other child – the one you did see – maybe she could feel all of that," she said quietly. "She must feel that maternal love, and grief, coming from you. Something this house ain't felt for a very long time."

"I don't need to be someone else's surrogate mother," Catherine said. "I need my Sarah back."

"But maybe this other child needs you," Delphine replied.

"What? What does she need? How can I possibly help this person who, by the way, doesn't seem to be looking for help. She seems intent on driving me insane."

"She could be lashing out in frustration," Delphine suggested. "Just as you thought Sarah might be doing. You kept calling her Sarah, right?"

"This is all insane," Catherine said, shaking her head. "I'm losing my mind."

"You are NOT losing your mind," Delphine said firmly. "I believe every word you're saying."

"Well then what am I supposed to do about it? Because I can't live this way."

Delphine took a deep breath, deciding whether to take the conversation further.

"You ever heard of Hoodoo?" she asked.

"You mean, like with voodoo dolls and black magic type stuff?" Catherine asked.

Delphine shook her head.

"That's voodoo. I'm talking about Hoodoo. And I guess you folks might say it's like magic. But it's real. Just as real as what you've been experiencing. It can help you harness the powers of this world. And the next."

She paused to see if Catherine seemed curious and took her lack of response as a sign to continue.

"Hoodoo's been passed down through my family for generations. Simply put, there are things out there that can be explained, and other things that cannot. Some in my family had the power of seeing things beyond our reality, others were able to hear them. And there's been some like you, who not only see and hear, but feel. You've been given a gift. Let me help you use it."

"I don't want this gift," Catherine replied.

"A spirit is calling you for help," Delphine said. "A child. She needs you. You need to help her."

"What if I don't want to help her?" Catherine said. "I just want my old life back. I want my Sarah back."

"I mean no disrespect, but life don't very much care about what you want," Delphine said. "And neither do the afterlife. These spirits are here because they're tormented, just like you. And they need to resolve something before they can move on."

Catherine shook her head and stood.

"Well, I can't help her," she said. "I can't even help myself. I'm sorry."

Delphine watched as Catherine stormed out of the room. She wanted to comfort her but knew the best thing she could do was give her new friend space and just be there for her when she needed it.

And she would definitely need it. Delphine knew firsthand how relentless the spirit world could be.

24

CATHERINE SPENT the bulk of the day pretending to be sick so she could avoid talking to anyone. She thought a lot about what Delphine had said to her and, while she wasn't ready to go all Hoodoo, her curiosity began to get the best of her.

If there's a spirit of a child in this house, that means a child died here.

Dale had told her the house had been in the family for generations, having been built during the mid-1800s. She imagined that there had probably been many deaths in the house or surrounding property in that time, and she knew that child deaths were very common at the turn of the century. But that was mostly caused by disease and infections. If what Delphine had said was right – that a spirit lingers in our existence because of something that is unresolved – then there may have been something more memorable than disease that killed the spirit haunting Catherine.

It was a cloudy early fall day, and the temperatures had dropped to be unseasonably cool. Dale took advantage of the more reasonable weather to work on the ramp. He was never one to just sit still, but since his daughter's death, he had made an art form of preoccupying his time. The alternative was to face the reality of what happened, and he just wasn't ready for that. After all, someone had to be strong. His wife was barely holding herself together. And now he had his father to deal with. He simply didn't have the luxury to grieve.

He had called Virgil again and the odd neighbor had agreed to help. The two men were both working on the framework when Catherine stepped outside. She was visibly stunned to see Virgil. She instinctively took a step back and Virgil responded with a suspicious stare. While he did seem less disarming doing carpentry with her husband, Catherine still got a strange feeling around him. Maybe it was just how she had originally met him. How she might subconsciously be associating him with her strange experiences by the boathouse. She admonished herself for judging him unfairly.

"Hi Virgil," she said with a smile.

Virgil quickly looked down, as if he was afraid to make eye contact.

"You boys doing okay out here?" she asked.

Dale stopped hammering and looked up at his wife.

"We're making a lot of progress," he said. "Are you feeling any better?"

With a pale complexion and bags under her eyes, she

certainly didn't look better. But she managed to put on a fake smile.

"I think I just needed to catch up on some sleep," she said. "Now I'm a little antsy. Need any help?"

Dale grinned at her.

"Some water would be great," he said.

"So, I'm fetching water for the men. I see," Catherine winked, disappearing into the house before Dale could defend his statement.

She returned shortly with two bottles of water and handed them to Dale and Virgil, who still avoided eye contact.

"Thank God for this break in the heat," she said, trying to maintain some small talk.

But she grew impatient quickly and after just a few minutes, got around to what was really on her mind.

"So, what all do y'all know about this house?" she asked. "Like, about its past and all?"

Virgil looked at Dale, clearly stunned by the question.

"Well, there's a question out of the blue," Dale teased. "I know it's been in the family forever. Before the Civil War it was a big plantation. One of the biggest in the areas. After the war, my ancestors supposedly split up the bulk of the land and gave it to their newly freed slaves. At least, that's the family story."

"It's not true?"

"Sounds too good to be true," Dale said. "Sounds to me like my ancestors literally whitewashed their guilt. Then again, I never looked into it, so maybe it is true."

"I bet a lot of people have died here over the years," she said, fishing.

"Probably," Dale said with a shrug.

"What do you think, Virgil?" she asked, directing the question to the visibly uncomfortable man.

He shook his head and pointed in the direction of his house.

"I live over there," he said. "My whole life. I don't know about here."

"Come on, you two," Catherine prodded playfully. "Play along. I'm bored and trying to entertain myself. Tell me what you've heard. Any rumors? Ghost stories?"

Virgil shook his head again, this time more vehemently. "You're not supposed to talk about dead people."

"I don't mean any disrespect to them," Catherine said. "But, come on. In this old house? There have to be some good ghost stories. Someone murdered. Or any kids that died."

"No. You're not supposed to talk about dead people," Virgil said adamantly before dropping his hammer and walking to the side of the house.

Catherine called out to him. "Virgil! I'm sorry!" She turned to Dale. "I didn't mean to upset him."

Dale shrugged.

"You never know with him," he said. "His mother was very strange. Hyper religious. Suspicious of everyone. She barely let Virgil out of the house. Lord knows what all she put in his head."

"I should go apologize," Catherine said.

"He'll be fine," Dale replied. "But Cat. What the hell is going on with these questions?"

"I'm just curious," she answered with a shrug.

"No. This is something else. Why are you asking about dead kids? Are you hearing things again? Are you imagining that Sarah's talking to you again?"

"Damnit, Dale," Catherine snapped. "Not everything is about that. I'm just trying to have a conversation."

"I don't believe you."

"How dare you!" she said. "I am sick and tired of your constant judgement."

"I'm not judging you, Cat."

"You're accusing me. That's the same thing."

"I'm sorry," he said. "You're right. And I'm sorry."

She sighed and knelt next to her husband.

"Honey, I know you're trying to protect me," she said. "But I have too much time on my hands here. All I do is think. About everything."

"Did something happen?" Dale asked without even thinking.

Catherine stood again.

"You're not even listening," she said. "Tell Virgil that I'm sorry I spooked him."

Afraid to say the wrong thing, Dale measured his next words carefully, but Catherine stormed back into the house before he could speak. He winced as the front door slammed shut.

CATHERINE STORMED BACK into the house but stopped when she spotted Henry in the parlor talking to someone. She tried to get a closer look at Henry and his guest without being seen. But Henry noticed her and abruptly spun his wheelchair toward her.

"Catherine, is that you?" he yelled out.

Catherine let out a sigh and stepped into the room. But she was surprised to see that Henry was alone.

Was he talking to himself? she wondered.

"There's a book on the top shelf I need you to get for me," he said, somehow managing to ask for help without really asking.

Catherine nodded, embarrassed that she had caught Henry in a private moment.

"Which book?" she asked as she walked closer.

"An old Louis L'Amour," he said. "I'm in the mood for a good western."

Catherine saw the Louis L'Amour novel on the shelf.

She pulled it down and handed him the tattered paperback. A rip in the cover had been taped up and several of the yellowed pages were dog-eared.

"Seems to be a favorite," she said as she handed it to him.

"That's Dale's handiwork," Henry said. "He read this book over and over as a kid. Was never good at taking care of things."

"There are a lot of old books here," Catherine said. "How old are some of these?"

"They've been here since before I was born," Henry said. "For all I know, they're painted into the shelves."

Catherine decided to try her luck with Henry.

"You grew up here, right? How much do you know about this house?" she asked. "There's got to be so much history."

"I ain't never heard of an old house that don't collect its share of secrets," Henry said. "I can't imagine this one's any different."

"Oooh. What kind of secrets?" Catherine asked. "Anything good?"

Henry looked at Catherine suspiciously.

"You're looking for something, ain't you?" he asked. "What are you suddenly so nosy about?"

"I'm just curious. And bored," she said. "Come on. You must have heard something. Like any ghost stories? Or murders? Maybe kids?"

"Okay, that's it," Henry said. "Here's all I got to say to you: Those are disturbing questions and even if I had an answer, they ain't none of your business."

Catherine was startled by his abruptness.

"I didn't mean anything by it," she stammered.

"If there are any secrets in these walls, and I ain't saying there is, then they are family secrets. And I don't care that you married into it, you ain't family."

"I'm sorry, Henry," she said. "I really meant no disrespect."

Henry sighed, calming himself down.

"Look. I get it," he said. "I know what you're doing. But take my advice and stop focusing on the past - either yours or anyone else's. Start looking forward. There ain't nothing but regrets, guilt and bad memories behind you."

"I just wanted to know if..."

"Chasing old ghosts is what got me in this contraption," he interrupted. "I get you're bored but find something else to do with your time. Try cooking. Maybe you can clean up in here. Do some yard work. I don't give a rat's ass. Just leave the past alone. For your own good."

He spun his chair around and rolled toward the door.

"Thanks for the book," he grumbled as he rolled out of sight.

Henry's reaction had the opposite of its intended effect and Catherine felt more resolved than ever to investigate the past. She hadn't been lying about being bored. Looking into the home's past did more than help her try and discover a ghost's past life. When she was investigating the house, she wasn't thinking about Sarah. She wasn't as worried about another haunting. It empowered her and gave her a sense of control, whether real or not. It gave her a sense of purpose, and she had latched on to it as if her sanity depended on it.

She turned back to the bookshelf, looking for

anything that could give a glimpse into the home's history.

Where would I store memories if I didn't want them staring me in the face? she asked herself.

She smiled as the answer dawned on her.

26

FOLLOWING A HUNCH, Catherine walked down the dark upstairs hallway, quickly scurrying past the abandoned room, until she reached a narrow door at the corridor's end. Much to her relief, it opened to a steep, narrow staircase that ascended into blackness. They were the stairs to the attic.

As she stared up into the darkness, her excitement of victory was quickly extinguished; replaced with the unfortunately familiar feeling of dread. She ran her hand over the walls on either side but was unable to find a light switch. So, Catherine took a deep breath and began to cautiously walk up the creaky steps. The blackness swallowed her whole in seconds, and she was unable to see anything. As one hand clutched the small wooden handrail, the other extended in front of her to feel her way through the darkness. As she climbed the steps, the only sounds were the creaks under her feet and the rapid pounding in her chest.

When her extended hand brushed against something

unexpectedly, she quickly recoiled, nearly tumbling backwards down the stairs. Regaining her foothold, she slowly extended her hand again. It was another door. She fumbled for the doorknob and turned it slowly, pushing it open.

Adrenaline surged as the door creaked open.

What am I doing? she thought. *Go back. Get a flashlight. This is stupid.*

But she ignored her better judgement and stepped inside. Something soft lightly brushed against her cheek and she flinched.

It's probably just a spiderweb, she rationalized.

She reached out slowly and waved her trembling hand through the blackness. Then she felt it again. But now she recognized it. It was a cotton drawstring for a lightbulb. Letting out a sigh of relief, she pulled the string chain, and the old filaments of the bulb flickered to life with a buzz. Long shadows stretched across the slatted floor as a dim yellow light revealed rows of shelves filled with boxes and keepsakes.

As Catherine stepped deeper into the room, the shadows shifted. Catherine gasped when something seemed to dart behind a distant shelf. She tried to shake it off, telling herself that her eyes were just playing tricks on her. She cautiously continued forward into the shadowy web.

A box on a top shelf seemed to move. Catherine stared at it to see if it would move again. And then it did. Just a slight shuffle, but it definitely moved.

Was it a sign? Was she supposed to see that box?

Catherine reached for it; her breath caught in her

throat. Just as she touched it, something shot out from behind it. Catherine screamed and fell backward as a mouse scurried away.

Catching her breath, Catherine stood back up and brushed herself off. The jolt released the tension and pulled her back into reality. She explored the shelves further, but now with less hesitation. The boxes were all labeled in black marker with things like "Old China" and "Baby Clothes." There were several old children's toys and a box or two of children's books that Catherine fought the urge to rifle through.

As she walked past the boxes, she didn't notice that the shelf behind her had begun to rock slowly. She turned just as the shelf began to shake violently, toppling boxes and trinkets to the ground. It began to fall directly toward her, but Catherine jumped out of the way just as it crashed to the ground.

Catherine sat on the wooden attic floor, petrified in fear. The hanging lightbulb began to sway, scattering frantic shadows across the room. She caught her breath and surveyed the damage. Several boxes had fallen. One box in particular had toppled over, and old photos were now scattered across the floor. She picked up a couple of photographs that had slid closest to her.

One was a photo of a beautiful young woman holding a baby. While she recognized neither of them, she assumed it was an infant Dale with his mother. Catherine smiled, but she also instantly felt a pang in her heart. The photo reminded her of when her Sarah was a baby. She remembered how much she loved holding her baby daughter. How light she was. How soft her skin was. How tight her little grip was around Catherine's finger. And, of course, that unmistakable baby scent. Catherine recalled all the hopes and dreams she had then for her new daughter. How she looked forward to watching her grow up, wondering where her life would take her. Never in a million years did she imagine it would all be yanked away.

Catherine wiped the tears from her eyes and reached for another photo. This was was a picture of a young girl around six or seven, with blonde hair and a beautiful smile. She was wearing a yellow dress and Catherine's heartbreak was instantly washed away by a feeling of dread. The girl in the photo was the same girl that had been haunting her.

"Who are you?" she asked out loud.

Something made her look up.

Standing right in front of her was the young girl in the photo. Except her skin was a ghostly gray and she was soaking wet. As water dripped from her into a puddle at her feet, her dead eyes stared intensely at Catherine, a single tear running down her cheek.

"Help me," she whispered through pale blue lips, her voice haunting and ethereal.

Catherine sat frozen. It took all her strength to utter a single word.

"How?"

The girl's eyes bore into Catherine, unmoving and unblinking.

"Help me," she said again, exactly as she had before.

A deep sadness washed over Catherine. Without even

knowing why, she began to cry and soon reached up to wipe the tears from her eyes.

Then the girl was gone.

Catherine stared at the empty space in front of her, trying to process what just happened.

She didn't realize the girl was now standing behind her, until a cold hand reached out and grabbed her shoulder.

27

CATHERINE WAS NO LONGER in the attic. Instead, she was standing in the sunlit backyard of the Devereux property, landscaped and maintained the way it must have once been. The little girl was there, giggling as she chased butterflies through the garden. She ran past Catherine and as Catherine turned around, she was suddenly standing in front of the boathouse.

Like the yard, the boathouse had also returned to its former glory, gleaming with a fresh coat of red paint. The dock next to it looked as if it had just been built.

Catherine followed the girl as she skipped to the boathouse and, standing behind her, watched as she slowly opened the door. Immediately, everything became dark and foreboding. Horror rooted Catherine to the spot as she stared at a shadowy mass pulsing and undulating against the far wall. Something, or someone, was trying to break free from it. The face of a woman pushed through the mass, straining to escape.

"Dru," the woman cried out, her hand stretching out to the little girl before the blackness swallowed her again. Then a sinister silhouette emerged from the mass. A man-like figure that slithered toward them.

The girl turned and fled, passing right through Catherine. Suddenly, it was as if Catherine had been swallowed up by the girl. She was now seeing everything through the child's terrified eyes. She raced around the dock, the monstrous figure chasing her. She felt a cold grip on her wrist, and she looked down, expecting to see a hand. Instead, a large black snake had coiled around her wrist, and it was slithering its way up her arm until it coiled around her neck. Catherine could feel the snake tighten its grip around her neck as its head moved in front of her and stared into her eyes. Then, baring its fangs, it lunged at her.

Catherine jolted back to reality in the attic, and she quickly scrambled away from the spot where the girl had stood. But she was gone. Catherine reached up to her throat to make sure she was okay. Panic and fear surged through her body.

What the hell just happened?

Her breath came in gasps as she tried to calm herself, her mind racing to make sense of it all. She looked at the photo again, studying the image of the girl. Who was she? Why was her photo in the attic? What had happened to her?

But those questions were soon replaced with others. Was it a hallucination? Was it a vision? Or was it just her imagination?

Am I losing my mind?

28

———

CATHERINE SAT on the edge of the bed, staring at the prescription bottle she was holding in her trembling hands. She pushed the lid down and twisted off the cap, pouring a couple of the tablets into her hand.

Maybe this will help, she wondered. *Maybe this is all in my mind.*

She wanted to believe that. She wanted to believe she could just make it go away. But she knew better. She knew in her heart it was real. At the very least, it was real to her. And she needed to see it through.

She closed her eyes, trying to shake the image of the pale gray girl staring at her. As terrifying as it was, she couldn't help but fixate on the tear rolling down the child's face. She thought about what Delphine had told her.

"They are here because they are tormented. They need to resolve something before they can move on."

She poured the pills back into the bottle and secured

the lid. As she set it on the nightstand, Dale walked into the room with a cup of tea.

"Here you go," he said. "This should help your headache."

"Thank you," she said.

"And sorry about earlier," he said.

Catherine nodded and Dale sat next to her on the side of the bed. The silence was awkward and tentative.

"I need to show you something," she finally said. "But you have to promise not to get mad."

"Uh-oh," he said. "Nothing good ever followed that sentence."

Catherine smiled nervously. Unable to look him in the eyes, she studied the floor.

"I went up into the attic this afternoon," she said.

Dale let out a sigh of disapproval.

"I know. But I did it and it's done," she continued. "And I found some old pictures."

She slipped her hand under the pillow and pulled out the photo of the girl in the yellow dress. Dale stared at it, puzzled.

"Who's this?" he asked.

"I was hoping you could tell me," she replied in disappointment.

Dale shrugged. "She doesn't look familiar to me," he said.

"Why would her picture be in the attic?" Catherine asked.

"Beats me," Dale said. "Maybe a cousin? When was it taken?"

"It doesn't say," Catherine replied. "But it looks old."

"Before my time, maybe?" Dale suggested.

Catherine let out a sigh, disappointed that Dale couldn't shed any light on the mysterious girl.

"Why do you care so much?" Dale asked.

Catherine wanted to tell him everything, but she already knew how he would react. He'd think she was losing her mind. At best, he'd panic and want to take her back to the treatment facility. But it could also be the final nail in the coffin of their tenuous marriage. He could finally get fed up and walk away. She knew she couldn't risk either. Instead, she pulled the other picture from under the pillow and handed it to Dale.

"I also found this," she said gently.

Dale studied the photo of the mother and baby.

"Who is it?" he said, his voice softening as if he really knew the answer.

"I think that baby is you," Catherine said. "And that's your mother."

Dale touched the image in the photograph, confused and bewildered by it. He looked at the way the woman was smiling, as if she was laughing.

"She looks so happy," Dale said, his voice almost a whisper.

He chuckled sadly. "I've never even seen a picture of her before," he said. "When she left I wasn't much older than this. Still a baby. I have no memory of her at all. And, after she left, Henry got rid of everything about her. All pictures. Everything. I wasn't allowed to ask questions. Even Doc wouldn't tell me much, out of respect for Henry's wishes. She just faded away. That sounds awful, doesn't it?"

Catherine reached out to wipe a tear from his face. She felt awful for opening up memories that he had clearly spent a lifetime repressing. Dale snapped up, remembering something.

"Hang on," he said, setting the photo down on the bed and went to his closet, pushing clothes to the side to expose the wall at the back of the closet. He felt around for a crack near the corner of the wall and pulled out a section to reveal a small hiding place.

"I cut out this little hideaway when I was a kid," he said. "Kept my treasures in it, not that I really had any. Except this."

He pulled out a folded, crinkled piece of paper, and walked back to Catherine.

"When I was about six, I snuck downstairs one night and spotted Henry in the kitchen. He was drunk as usual, but he was holding this paper, sobbing. Then he crumpled it up and threw it away. I hid until he left, then dug through the trash to see what he had been reading."

He handed the piece of paper to Catherine.

"It was a letter from my mother. She must have sent it a few months after she left, and he had kept it up until that night."

"Oh my God," Catherine said, scanning over the letter. It was typewritten on stationary from the Hilton Chicago.

"I'd read it all the time, over and over. I don't know why. Maybe because it was all I had of her? Maybe I kept hoping it would say something different? But then Henry sent me off to boarding school and I eventually just forgot about it."

Catherine read it out loud.

"Dear Henry and my darling Dale, I can't expect you to ever understand why I had to leave. There are just too many memories haunting me, keeping me from being the wife and mother you both deserve. I've relocated in the Midwest and am attempting to start a new life. Please don't look for me. And please go on with your lives. Know that I think about you both every day and take solace in knowing you are both better off without me. I'll love you always, Susan."

Catherine set the paper down, unsure of what to say.

He picked up the photo and looked at the image of his mother again.

"I always blamed Henry for chasing her off, and for stealing her from me," Dale said. "But now, after... you know...I can see it a little differently. I'd always just seen a drunk dad, but he was also a grieving husband. He'd lost his wife, and it clearly broke him."

He looked up at Catherine, tears in his eyes. "I don't want that to happen to me. To us."

"Oh, Dale. I'm so sorry," Catherine said.

"You're my family," Dale said. "You're all I have."

He broke down, letting out pain that had been buried for years. Catherine opened her arms, and he fell into them, sobbing.

29

THE NEXT MORNING, Catherine stood at the living room window, watching Dale work furiously on the ramp. He was working alone now, as Virgil had left after Catherine's questions and refused to return.

Even though Catherine had wanted to ask Henry questions about the girl in the photo, Dale talked her out of it. He told her he would bring it up. It would probably go over better, coming from him. Remembering Henry's comment about her not really being family, she reluctantly agreed. He convinced her that it would serve no other purpose than to aggravate him more. Even though Catherine knew her husband was reacting from a conditioned fear, she knew he was right.

They spent the rest of the evening alone, sharing a vulnerable tenderness for the first time in a long time. Catherine had even fallen asleep in his arms.

However, her peaceful slumber didn't last long and the recurring nightmares that had haunted her for months woke her in the middle of the night. She lay staring at the ceiling, afraid to return to the nightmares but also preoccupied with everything she had taken in. And what she could do about it.

When Dale woke up at daybreak for his morning run, she pretended to be asleep. But when he didn't return an hour later, Catherine got dressed and went downstairs. Henry and Delphine were nowhere to be found, so Catherine made a pot of coffee and took a cup into the parlor. That's when she heard the hammering from the front of the house.

For a minute, she watched him work furiously. From the determination on his face, she knew he was working through his frustration and guilt. She decided it was best to leave him alone. Besides, she had other plans.

Catherine finished her coffee and quietly opened the side kitchen door. She crept outside, being careful to remain hidden from Dale, and snuck around to the trail into the woods. She needed to go back to the boathouse. As much as she hated what she might encounter, she knew the boathouse somehow held the key to figuring out what the girl wanted from her.

It was the first really cloudy day of their visit, and everything was shrouded in an ominous pale gray tone. Gusts of wind shook the trees and blew leaves and pine needles through the air. When she arrived at the pond, white caps formed on the windswept water. The boathouse sat menacingly on the shore, dark and brooding. Catherine stared at it, gathering her courage.

"Okay, what now?" she muttered to no one.

Something in the boathouse window caught her attention. There appeared to be someone inside the boathouse looking out at her. Catherine's breath caught in her throat. It was a little girl.

She looked back to make sure Dale hadn't followed her. And when she turned back around, the girl in the boathouse was gone. Immediately, her determination shifted to self-doubt. She began to question everything again. She convinced herself that she had imagined it seeing someone. That it was just an illusion caused by reflections in the window.

Still, she found herself walking slowly toward the boathouse, afraid of what she would find. Almost hoping something or someone would pull her back. But she soon found herself standing in front of the boathouse door. She took a deep breath and gathered every ounce of courage she could muster, then slowly turned the handle and pushed the door open, taking a step back in anticipation.

Catherine glanced around inside. The water lapped loudly against the wooden walls and dock. The entire boathouse moaned and creaked as it swayed against the waves. The rising humidity seemed to heighten the intense odor of the dank air that sat in the decaying structure.

Catherine took a single step inside, peering into the shadows.

"Hello?" she asked quietly.

There was no response.

She took another step, looking toward the back of the boathouse where she had seen the shadowy figure before. There was nothing.

Catherine let out a sigh.

"Where are you?" she asked.

Half disappointed and half relieved that nothing happened, she turned to walk back out. Finally, stepping on to the wet grass and pulling the door shut.

Then something caught her attention. There was a glistening near the water's edge next to the boathouse. She walked over to it and knelt to get a better look. It was nothing more than wet stones catching the light that dodged through the swaying trees.

The only problem was the sky was covered in dark clouds. There was no light.

"This is crazy," she muttered.

And then, just a few feet from shore, a few bubbles rose to the water's surface. She leaned forward, squinting to see into the dark water. Something slowly began to come into focus. Catherine gasped, frozen in fear.

It was the decayed, ghastly body of the girl, floating just beneath the surface. Her eyes were shut, and she appeared to be sleeping peacefully.

Then the girl's eyes sprang open. They were bloodshot and yellow and staring directly at Catherine. Her decaying arm lunged out of the water and grabbed Catherine by the wrist, trying to yank her down to her. Catherine struggled to free herself, falling backwards then quickly scrambling to her feet.

The girl was gone. It happened so quickly that the terror it brought only began to show itself afterward. Catherine touched the wrist that had been grabbed. It was freezing cold, but bone dry. She struggled to catch her breath. Tears filled her eyes.

This is NOT my imagination. I am NOT losing my mind.

But if it was real, what did it all mean?

Her terror quickly transformed into a frustrated anger.

"What do you want from me?" she yelled into the water.

30

CATHERINE SPENT the rest of the day successfully dodging any questions about her day. Dale, exhausted from working on the ramp all day, called it a night early. Henry soon followed, retiring to his room with the Louis L'Amour paperback. Once she was satisfied both men were down for the night, Catherine headed to Delphine's room.

She knocked on the open door and Delphine, sitting in a small chair in front of a vanity, waved her in with a smile.

"Well, this is a first," she said. "Come in, child."

Catherine walked into the room, surveying the clutter of books, talismans, and shelves of small bottles. The walls were adorned with crucifixes of various sizes and styles, as well as many other odd charms and symbols that Catherine didn't recognize.

Delphine patted the bed for Catherine to sit down.

"To what do I owe this pleasure?" she asked.

Catherine immediately began to share everything

that had happened over the past two days. From the trip to the attic to the vision by the pond. The words poured out of her. She had been dying to talk to someone about it, and Delphine was the only one who would listen without judgement.

"It's like she is showing me all this for a reason," Catherine said. "But I just can't make sense of it."

Delphine studied the picture of the young girl.

"But you're still not sure who she is?" she asked.

Catherine shook her head. "No. But I can't imagine there would be a picture of her stored in the attic if she wasn't somehow attached to this family. Dale said he'd ask Henry, but I think he's honestly too afraid. Do you recognize her?"

Delphine handed the picture back.

"I fear this is before I was employed here."

She studied Catherine. She could see the panicked worry on her face. The circles under her eyes from lack of sleep. The nervous way she patted her foot.

"But I may be able to help," Delphine said. "However, you have to be sure it's what you want."

"I just want it to end," Catherine said.

Delphine hesitated and shook her head.

"Please, Delphine," Catherine pleaded. "I'm losing my mind."

Delphine nodded and pulled a small wooden box from a shelf, filling it with various items.

"Your conscious mind is blocking what the spirit child is trying to tell you. I can help you open the gate to the other side."

She turned to face Catherine. Her normally gentle face had hardened in a seriousness that jolted Catherine.

"Are you okay with that?" Delphine asked.

Catherine's eyes welled up with tears. She wiped them away as she nodded.

"I don't think I have a choice."

31

DELPHINE CLIMBED THE ATTIC STAIRS, turning the light on and motioning for Catherine to follow. The two women walked through the rows of shelves to the open space where Catherine had fallen earlier.

"You sit right there," she said, motioning to the floor covered in photographs. "Move those out of the way."

Delphine sat opposite her and, after clearing the area between them, began to carefully remove the contents of the box: a small black candle, a stick of incense, a small brass cup, a box of matches, a small burlap bag and a small wooden object. Catherine stared at the object. It seemed to be hand carved into the general shape of a human, but with no details or features.

"It's better if you do the ritual yourself, but I'll walk you through it step by step," Delphine explained.

"Is it going to hurt?" Catherine asked.

Delphine gave her a wink and a smile, not completely reassuring Catherine.

"Take the matches and light the candle first," Delphine instructed.

Catherine's nervous fingers fumbled with the matches. She ran it over the striking surface several times before it finally sparked. She held the flame to the wick of the candle, transferring the flame.

"Good," Delphine said. "Now blow out the match and use the candle to light the tip of the incense."

Catherine did as she was told, and the tip of the incense began to glow a brilliant red and a stream of white smoke began to slowly writhe upward in the air.

"Place the incense in the brass cup," Delphine said. "This will help clear the air and open your senses. Now open the burlap bag and take out a little bit of the powder at a time, making a circle between us."

Catherine reached in the bag with one hand, pinching some of the dark red, sand-like powder between her fingers and sprinkling it into a circle.

"What does this do?"

"It keeps everything contained inside of it. Helps concentrate the power."

Catherine finished creating the circle and set the bag aside.

"Did you bring the picture of the girl?" Delphine asked.

Catherine nodded, pulling the photograph from her back pocket.

"Place it in the middle of the circle, then place the wooden talisman on top of it," Delphine said.

Again, Catherine did as instructed. Delphine shut her eyes and began to quietly recite an incantation.

"What should I be doing?" Catherine said.

"I need you to hush, child," Delphine said. "Stare at that picture while I do my business."

Catherine nodded and Delphine returned to her quiet incantation. Catherine stared at the photo. Losing herself in the large, sad eyes of the child.

Delphine finally finished and nodded at Catherine.

"Take your talisman and hold it over the candle flame, then sprinkle a bit more powder on it."

Catherine picked up the wooden figure and held it over the flame, reaching into the pouch and pinching a bit more of the red powder. As she sprinkled the powder, it hit the flame and sparked. Catherine gasped and then watched as a deep blue smoke rose from the candle, enveloping the talisman.

Delphine quietly repeated her chant again and then, without ceremony, pinched out the candle's flame with her fingers. Then she folded Catherine's fingers over the talisman and held her hand tight.

"Keep this talisman with you then, tonight, place it under your pillow," Delphine explained. "It will help guide you to the other side."

"What will I find there?" Catherine asked with a whisper.

"That is a journey you will need to take on your own," Delphine said. "But she will be there with you."

"I'm trusting you, Delphine," she said.

"Trust yourself," Delphine replied softly. "This will free your body, your mind and your soul. Only then can you be truly free to travel to the other side."

"But I'll be able to come back when I want, right?" Catherine asked.

Delphine took her hand into her own.

"When you travel to the other side, there are never any guarantees," she said. "Don't do this unless you are truly ready."

32

CATHERINE STARED in the bathroom mirror, studying the dark circles under her tired eyes. Her body, numb from exhaustion, was also filled with the buzzing of anxiety.

What am I doing? she thought.

She stared at the talisman in her hand, trying to build up courage when a loud knock on the bathroom door jolted her back to the present.

"Hey, Babe," Dale mumbled. "You coming to bed?"

"In a minute," she replied, trying a little too hard to sound normal.

"You take your sleeping pills?" he asked.

Catherine stared at the herb packet.

"Was just about to."

Delphine's warning echoed in her mind.

When you travel to the other side, there are never any guarantees.

She took a deep breath and let it out with a sigh.

She climbed into bed where Dale already lay, facing away from her. She discreetly placed the talisman under her pillow, facing in the opposite direction. She nuzzled up to him and gently kissed him on the cheek.

"I love you, Dale," she said quietly.

Dale shifted around and looked at her with a smile.

"I love you, too."

He wanted to ask what brought about this sudden burst of affection, but he stopped himself. He knew that would probably just lead to an argument. Instead, he leaned up and kissed her lightly on the lips.

She wanted to cling to this moment. To never let it go. But she knew what she had to do. She smiled at him then turned to switch off the bedside lamp. As she lay on her side away from her husband, she slid her hand under the pillow to make sure the talisman was still there. For the first time in days, her eyelids felt heavy, and she found herself being pulled into sleep.

Her eyes shot open with a jolt. She slowly propped herself up on her elbows and looked around as her eyes adjusted to the dark. Then she gasped in horror.

Paralyzed with terror, she stared at the foot of the bed. It was the girl. She was soaking wet, her hair matted onto her pallid face. Her dress was faded and smeared in black mud. Catherine tried to back away, but she was literally frozen in fear, her body refusing to cooperate. The girl's blank stare fixed on Catherine, and she began to step closer.

Splish.

Splish.

Splish.

The young girl's wet footsteps echoed as she moved closer until she was inches from Catherine's face. Her ghastly gray skin was wet and rotted. Her black eyes were void of any life as she stared right through Catherine. Catherine's heart thundered in her chest as she struggled to breathe.

Then the whispers began. At first, they were faint, distant murmurs, but they quickly grew louder and more aggressive.

Catherine watched helplessly as the girl extended a clammy hand toward her. Water dripped from her arm and Catherine felt the cold droplets splash onto her chest. She strained to move, to even turn her head, but she was completely paralyzed. She could do nothing as the cold, damp hand settled over her face. The smell was horrific, like rancid water and decaying flesh, and Catherine was plunged into a suffocating darkness.

33

CATHERINE OPENED HER EYES. She was no longer in bed. She wasn't even in the house. Instead, Catherine stood near the edge of the pond. A gentle breeze stirred up tiny waves, breaking the reflection of the full moon into ripples of soft light. The terror that had gripped her so tightly was gone and she felt a sense of peace and calm. The faint sound of a humming child drew her gaze. Her head turned with a slow, heavy movement.

The little girl was no longer the decayed monster at the foot of her bed. She was now a vision of innocence, smiling in her bright yellow dress, playing hopscotch. But not on the grass. She was playing on the pond's surface. She hopped in slow motion over invisible squares, her humming fading in and out.

Catherine felt another presence and looked beyond the boathouse to the hydrangea bushes that sat on an incline. She could make out the faded outline of someone watching in the shadows.

Aware of movement behind her, she turned back

toward the pond, her movement still slow and heavy. But the girl had vanished. In the spot where she had been playing, a black mass floated ominously over the dark waters. Catherine squinted, trying to make out what it was. Then, like a gust of frigid air, the mass surged toward her, passing through her in an icy blast.

Catherine gasped for breath. Her body felt different. Cold. And wet. She realized she was soaked, and a damp chill shot through her body. She looked around for the black mass and thought it had disappeared at first. Then she saw it. Pulsing and writhing underwater. It appeared to be struggling with something - or someone. Bubbles began to float up to the surface.

Without warning, an unseen force seized Catherine by the back of her hair, yanking her head back. She was flung to the ground, but instead of hitting the wet grass, she plunged into the black water. She began to sink, and she thrashed to fight her way back to the surface. But something was holding her down. She began to feel weak and even more disoriented as the dark, murky water began to swallow her.

She fought against it but then felt a hand gripping her, holding her under. Her eyes snapped open, and she stared up through the water's surface. Daylight filtered down, and she could see the shadowy shape of a man pinning her underwater. She fought desperately, turning her focus to his arm holding her down. She found herself fixating on it. It began to pulse and move until, to Catherine's horror, it transformed into a black snake.

A muffled scream from the surface broke her trance.

Someone was running toward them. Catherine was able to make out her face. It was Dale's mother.

And then she heard the young girl's pleading voice.

"Help me, Mommy!"

Dale's mother responded.

"Dru!"

"Mommy!" the girl pleaded again.

Dale woke with a jolt as Catherine thrashed beside him. She was drenched in sweat, but still asleep, apparently trapped in a nightmare.

"Nooooo!" she cried out in her sleep.

Dale shook her gently.

"Cat. Sweetheart," he said.

When she didn't respond, he sat up and began to shake her harder.

"Cat!"

Catherine's eyes shot open. They were solid white. Dale jumped back in horror as water started to gargle out of his wife's mouth.

"No!" he yelled, as he grabbed her again, trying to shake her awake.

Still being held underwater, Catherine could feel something shaking her. She flinched as a bright light washed over her and a series of images flashed before her eyes:

Bubbles rising in dark waters toward the dark silhouette of a man.

Dirt being tossed over a body.

A gold, heart-shaped locket pulsing and throbbing like a real heart.

A snake slithering down a thick honey locust tree, leaving thorny spikes in its wake.

The earth beneath the tree dissolving into blood, then rising up, enveloping the trunk until a branch partially broke, creating a grotesque shape.

Catherine clenched her eyes shut as Dale continued to try and wake her. She gasped for air but couldn't breathe. Dale straddled her, panic etched on his face, unsure what to do.

And then Catherine opened her eyes again. They were normal. "Oh, thank God," Dale said, pulling her into a hug, unaware of her struggle to breathe.

Catherine writhed, fighting for air.

"Are you okay?" he asked. "What's wrong?"

Catherine began to panic.

Why can't I breathe?

"Cat?" Dale's voice was a lifeline.

Suddenly, she sucked in a deep breath. Then another, as air filled her empty lungs.

"Are you okay?" he asked again, his voice shaking.

Catherine nodded. Her entire body buzzed from the panic. Remnants of the vision began to fade, and she became more aware of her surroundings, aware of Dale for the first time. Tears streamed down her face as she clung to him.

"I saw everything," she whispered between gasps. "Oh, my God."

"What? Saw what?" Dale asked. "Honey, you're scaring me."

She looked at Dale as the realization of what she saw sunk in.

"The girl. In the photo," she said. "Her name was Dru."

Dale was still confused.

"What are you talking about?"

Catherine locked eyes with him.

"Her name is Dru. I think she is your sister."

Dale shook his head.

"You're not making any sense."

More memories of the vision flooded her mind, and she was overcome with horror.

"Oh God. He killed her," she said. "I saw him."

"Killed who?" Dale asked, more worried than confused. "Honey, you had a nightmare."

"He killed her," she repeated. "He drowned her. I saw it."

Dale let out an exasperated sigh. "Honey, it was a nightmare."

"He killed her. I was there. He killed her and he buried her. And your mom was there."

Dale grabbed Catherine by her shoulders. "Honey, you're awake now. Everything's okay."

He tried to pull her close, but she pushed him away.

"It wasn't a dream. I saw it. It was under a tree," she

said emphatically. But the creeping reality of consciousness began to erode her certainty. "It couldn't have been."

She began to calm down and this time, when Dale pulled her close, she fell into his arms. He stroked her hair, murmuring soothing words.

"It's okay," he said. "Everything's okay."

"It was real," she muttered against his chest. "You have to believe me. It was real."

34

Dr. Mason walked down the stairs and joined Dale, Henry and Delphine in the parlor. Dale, who had been pacing nervously ever since Dr. Mason arrived, finally stopped, looking up at the doctor for a verdict. Dr. Mason smiled and gently waved him down.

"Everything's okay," he said quietly. "I gave her a sedative and she's fast asleep."

"If everything is okay then why are we all up in the middle of the night?" Henry grumbled, clearly not happy about this nocturnal interruption. Dale glared at his father, ready to let into him, but Delphine motioned at him to let it go.

"She most likely had some sort of seizure," Dr. Mason said. "She doesn't seem to remember any of it. It's all a bit out of my area of expertise, but I recommend she gets some tests done."

Dale was relieved to hear that she didn't remember any of it.

That must mean it was definitely all a nightmare, right?

He had only told Mason and Henry that she was saying all kinds of gibberish that didn't make sense. He didn't want to tell them the actual things she said. He knew that would only throw fuel on the fire. Besides, it was all clearly nightmares fueled by all the fragments she had been putting in her brain. That picture of the little girl. The conversation about his mother. Knowing she's already forgotten it, only helped to support his nightmare theory.

"What kind of tests?' Dale asked, pulling himself back into the conversation. "What's wrong with her?"

Dr. Mason shrugged. "From your description, it sounds like a clonic seizure, but it's really hard to tell. All kinds of things could trigger it. Low blood sodium. An infection. Lack of sleep."

"What about if she's crazy?" Henry asked.

"I swear to God," Dale said, ready to pounce.

"Mental illness can be connected," Dr. Mason said. "Another reason why I recommend more tests. Unfortunately, we don't necessarily have the right tools to do that here."

"Well, then take her to where she can be tested," Henry said.

"Can you try not being an asshole for just a second?" Dale snapped.

"Don't you talk to me that way," Henry yelled back.

Dale tried to regain his composure. "We'll leave right away," he assured Mason.

∽

Upstairs, Catherine lay in bed listening to the muffled voices arguing downstairs. Tears streamed down her face. She hadn't told Dr. Mason the truth about anything. She didn't tell him about the visions and about the Hoodoo ritual. She knew that would only make her seem more insane.

She opened her trembling hand, looking at the pills Dr. Mason had given her. She wanted to sleep. She wanted to escape this nightmare. But if Dale was planning on taking her away, she didn't have much time.

Catherine stuffed the pills under the mattress as she plotted her next move.

35

CATHERINE PRETENDED to be asleep when Dale returned to the room, keeping her breath measured and even. She could feel his gaze looking over her and then the mattress shift as he lay down next to her. She remained motionless, listening for the rhythmic sounds of his movements that signaled he had finally fallen asleep. As soon as the darkness of the night began to fade into the soft gray of pre-dawn, she slipped out of bed, got dressed, and tiptoed out of the room.

She was surprised to find Delphine sitting in the kitchen. Catherine hesitated. She wanted to tell Delphine everything, but knew she had to act before everyone else woke up.

"You learned something, didn't you?" Delphine asked.

Catherine nodded.

"Now I just need to prove it," she said.

"Did you tell Dale?" Delphine asked.

"I tried, but he thought it was all a nightmare. And

then he called Dr. Mason. You're the only one who believes me."

"This can be a hard thing for people to believe. Or even comprehend."

"Delphine. Her name was Dru. And I saw Dale's mother. The one from the picture. And Dru called her Mommy."

"This girl is Dale's sister?"

"Did you know he had a sister?" Catherine asked.

"You know more than I do. Especially now. But if Henry buried the memory of his wife, he could have just as easily buried any memory of a daughter. You need to talk to him."

"I will. But there's something else," Catherine said. "She was murdered."

"The girl?"

Catherine nodded. "I saw it. Someone drowned her. And buried her."

"Who?"

"I didn't see his face," Catherine admitted. "But I think I know how to find her. I need to find her. I think that's what she's wanted."

Then she noticed the luggage sitting next to Delphine. All of the urgency fell away in a heartbeat.

"What's that?" she asked, afraid of the answer.

Delphine smiled and Catherine's heart dropped. She sat down at the table.

"Why?" Catherine asked.

Delphine reached out and squeezed Catherine's hand.

"They found the talisman under your pillow," she said.

"He can't just fire you," Catherine exclaimed.

"No, Child. It's okay," Delphine said. "This was my idea. I offered to leave to spare him the decision I know he'd never make."

"I don't understand."

"It's time for me to go," she said. "I've got my own family to tend to. Besides, I think I'm creating more problems than I should be."

"No. This is all my fault," Catherine said.

"It's nobody's fault," Delphine said. "I will be fine and so will you."

"I need your help," Catherine pleaded.

Delphine squeezed Catherine's hand again.

"Miss Catherine, you've got this. Follow your instincts. Dru is guiding you now. You're going to be okay."

Catherine nodded, unconvinced.

"But I need you to promise me that you'll finish this. For that spirit child."

Delphine patted her heart.

"Remember. Trust yourself," she said. "You are NOT going insane. Now, go. Before the whole house wakes up."

Catherine squeezed Delphine's hand back then stood, heading out the door. Neither woman noticed the piece of paper that had fallen out of her pocket and was now lying on the kitchen floor.

36

A LIGHT RAIN began to fall as Catherine trudged through the woods. This time, she didn't take the detour to the boathouse. Instead, she scoured the forest in search of a particular tree. The tree with thorny spikes and the broken branch.

She followed her instincts, trusting that Dru would guide her path. She was so fixated on the trees, she almost didn't notice the barbed wire fence blocking her path. She would have missed it entirely if it weren't for the rusted tin sign attached to it.

NO TRESPASSING. KEEP OUT. VIOLATORS WILL BE SHOT.

Ignoring the sign, Catherine carefully lifted one strand of the barbed wire and squeezed through the gap, continuing her search for the tree.

Dru is buried underneath that tree, she thought. *She wouldn't have shown it to me if it didn't mean anything.*

How it would help her identify the killer was still unknown, but Catherine was certain that the answers

could all be found there. She no longer fought any
doubts. No longer questioned her sanity. She was
steadfast on this mission and felt completely certain she
was closing in on the truth.

She spent an hour scouring through the woods. The
rain had begun to fall steadily, and she was soaked to the
bone. She wiped her wet hair from her face and surveyed
the area around her, realizing she was within eyesight of
what must be Virgil's house.

It was more decrepit than Henry's place, but it
seemed to be less a product of neglect and more the way
it always had been. Instead of ivy-covered statues and
water fountains, the backyard was littered with old tires
and abandoned appliances. Most of the paint on the
small wood-paneled house had either flaked away or was
covered in moss and mold. The whole structure seemed
to be on the verge of toppling over.

But Catherine wasn't interested in the house. She
needed to find the tree. She turned back to face the
woods, trying to decide which way to explore. Darker
rain clouds had begun to roll in, blocking most of the
sunlight.

"I know you're here," she muttered.

She was so fixated on the tree, she didn't hear Virgil
walk up behind her.

"You ain't supposed to be here," he said.

His voice startled her, and she spun around to find
Virgil standing five feet away, holding a rusted garden till
in front of him as a weapon.

"Virgil," Catherine said. "It's me. Catherine. Dale's
wife."

"You're on private property," he continued. "You need to go."

His tone was matter of fact, but Catherine could see the anger in his eyes.

"I'm just looking for a tree," she said. "Maybe you can help me."

"Go NOW!" Virgil yelled.

The burst of anger startled Catherine. It also made her see him in a different light.

"You know the tree I'm talking about, don't you?" Catherine asked.

It was clearly more than an accusation and she noticed how Virgil twitched at the mention of the tree.

He knows something.

"Just go away," Virgil said. "I already done called the police."

"Good!" Catherine exclaimed, switching her demeanor to match his hostility. "It'll save me the trouble."

Thunder clapped and the rain began to fall harder. Catherine was so drenched, she no longer even noticed. Virgil was also getting soaked but didn't seem to care. Assuming he was all bark and no bite, Catherine decided to just walk past him, but he planted his feet, holding his ground, his grip on the garden till tightening.

"Go back home," he said. "You're not supposed to be here."

"Why?' Catherine asked. "Is there something you don't want me to find?"

Virgil shook his head. She could tell he was getting frustrated.

"Go away. Now," he said, growing increasingly agitated.

But Catherine, emboldened that she may have found Dru's killer, only grew more aggressive.

"You did it, didn't you?" she accused.

Virgil looked at Catherine in shock and confusion. He began to panic, rocking back and forth.

"You're supposed to mind your own business," he said.

"She was a little girl," Catherine said. "Why would you do that?"

Virgil rocked back and forth more violently as he became more frustrated and angrier.

"Mama said be quiet," he said loudly. "Mind your own business."

For the first time, Catherine felt his desperation, and began to worry that she could be his next victim.

"Virgil. Put down the till," she said.

"You GO!" Virgil yelled.

He swung the till at her. She could feel the air brush her face as he barely missed.

Fortunately, she could see a police car pulling into the driveway. Catherine raised her hands in surrender and watched the police officer get out of the car and start looking at the front of the house.

"Virgil, put down the garden till," she yelled, hoping to get the officer's attention.

It worked. Sergeant Dan Wilkerson saw the two people in the woods and began to walk towards them.

"Virgil?" Wilkerson yelled, squinting in the direction. "What the hell?"

Virgil snapped his head around to see the officer but quickly turned his attention back to Catherine.

"Make her go away."

Sergeant Wilkerson came up beside them, one hand on his pistol holster.

"I'm sorry, officer," Catherine said. "I have a good reason for being here."

"Virgil, put down the till," Wilkerson said.

Virgil held it away, out of Wilkerson's reach.

"She is trespassing," Virgil said.

"I am," Catherine said. "But not on purpose. I got lost. I was looking for a tree. I needed to prove something."

"And what's that?"

Catherine looked at Virgil, his face pinched in disapproval of the conversation.

"Ask Virgil," she said. "He knows."

Wilkerson turned to Virgil for an answer.

He shook his head violently and held the garden till in front of him.

"No! No! No!" he yelled.

"Virgil," Wilkerson yelled. "Put that down! Now!"

37

VIRGIL GLARED AT CATHERINE, then threw the till to the ground with a huff.

"I ain't hurt no one," he said, staring at Catherine. "Liar!"

"Who hurt who?" Wilkerson asked. "Someone better start talking. Quick."

"I'm looking for a tree," Catherine tried to explain, turning to Virgil. "THE tree."

"You can't be here!" Virgil yelled.

"Everyone stop," Sergeant Wilkerson said. "Someone needs to start explaining what the hell is going on."

"If I can find the tree, I can find the body," Catherine said.

"Whoa, whoa, whoa," Wilkerson said. "The body? What body? What the hell are you talking about, lady?"

"This is my house," Virgil said. "Make her go."

"Virgil, I need you to take a deep breath, okay?" Wilkerson said. "I need her to answer some questions first."

170 DAVID K. WILSON

From the way he spoke to Virgil, it was clear it wasn't the first time he had dealt with him.

"Why don't we all go back to my car and get out of the rain?" Wilkerson suggested. "We can talk there. Ma'am, how did you get here?"

"I walked," she said, pointing down toward the path. "I'm staying at Henry Devereux's house. I'm his daughter-in-law."

The officer nodded with a grin.

"You're Dale's wife?" he asked. "Come on. Let's go back to the car."

"He killed her. I know it," Catherine said, pointing at Virgil.

"Killed who?" Wilkerson asked.

"Dru," Catherine said. "Dru Devereux"

"Who?" Wilkerson asked.

"You drowned her in the pond," Catherine yelled at Virgil, growing angrier. "Why don't you just admit it?"

Wilkerson stood between the two, holding out his arms to keep them apart.

"Dru Devereux," he said, confirming what he heard.

"Mind your own business," Virgil muttered. He repeated it over and over, shaking his head and looking at the ground. "Mind your own business. Mind your own business."

"He killed her. I saw him," Catherine said. "And I can prove it. He buried her out there."

"What do you mean, 'you saw him'?" Wilkerson asked. "You're talking about Dru Devereux. Right?"

"Yes!" Catherine was relieved that he knew what she was talking about. "He held her down in the water. And then he buried her body under a tree with thorns all over it. And, and a broken branch. It's here. I'm sure of it."

"Ma'am, Dru Devereux died over thirty years ago," Wilkerson said. "How could you have seen it?"

"I'm not crazy," she said, realizing how she sounded.

"Why don't you come have a seat in my car?" Wilkerson said. "I can write it all down. Okay?"

She could tell he was treating her differently now. The same way she had treated Virgil when he first came up to them.

"Virgil, why don't you go sit down on your porch while I talk to this lady, okay?" Wilkerson said.

"She is trespassing," Virgil said.

"I know," Wilkerson replied. "I'll take care of it, okay?"

Virgil snorted and stomped off to his porch.

"Stay where I can see you, Virgil," Wilkerson said as he put an arm around Catherine and steered her toward his patrol car.

38

WHEN DALE WOKE UP, he was surprised to see Catherine's side of the bed already empty. He felt sure the sedative Dr. Mason had given her would have knocked her out a lot longer. He dressed quickly but froze when he saw the photos sitting on Catherine's bedside. He picked up the photo of the girl, remembering what Catherine had said during the night.

What was the name she had said? he asked himself. *Dru?*

He also remembered something else Catherine had said. That Dru was his sister. He grabbed both photos and headed downstairs to find his wife.

～

Expecting to find her sipping coffee in the kitchen, he tried there first. But the room was empty. Then he tried the parlor. But instead of Catherine, he found Henry staring out the bay window into the yard.

"Have you seen Catherine?" he asked flatly, not yet in the mood to deal with his dad after the argument they had during the night.

But Henry had different plans. He spun around and held up the letter from Dale's mother.

"Where did this come from?" Henry asked.

"How did you get it?" Dale countered.

"This wasn't meant for you," Henry snapped.

"Where did you find it?" Dale asked.

"Lying on the kitchen floor."

"Is Catherine in there?" Dale asked, turning toward the kitchen.

"I threw this away years ago!" Henry yelled.

Dale turned back around and snatched it out of his hands. "And I pulled it out of the trash."

"You had no right," Henry growled.

"You had no right," Dale snapped back. "You ran her off and then hid everything about her away from me? My own mother? I was a child!"

"Be careful," Henry warned, his tone darkening. "You don't know what you're talking about."

"You're right! I don't know," Dale shouted. "I don't know anything because you would never tell me!"

He shoved the picture of Dru in Henry's face.

"Who's this?" Dale asked.

Henry's face went pale as a ghost.

"Where? How?" he stammered.

"Is it true?" Dale said. "Is this my sister?"

"Where did you get this?" Henry asked. His voice was quieter now.

"Is it true?" Dale yelled furiously.

Henry snatched the picture out of Dale's hands and spun his wheelchair around, turning his back to Dale and accidentally kicking the Tiffany lamp in the process. It flickered before going dark.

Dale demanded his father turn around and talk to him. But Henry didn't respond. Dale saw his shoulders slump. He slowly turned the wheelchair around; tears were streaming down his face.

"Her name was Dru," he said, his voice much softer now. "She was about seven years older when you were born."

"And you never told me?" Dale yelled back, his fury still raging.

"I didn't know how," Henry said. There was no fight left in him. "Or when. And then it just got easier to say nothing."

"Not even now?" Dale continued. "With what I'm going through now? You didn't think this would be a nice-to-know?"

"What would it have mattered?" Henry asked.

Dale stared at his father. "I would at least know that you could understand. That you went through the same thing."

Henry's temper resurfaced quickly.

"You wanted to bond over it?" he sneered.

Dale resisted the urge to snap back. He paced the room trying to process his anger as well as all the information that was just thrown at him.

"How did she die?" he finally asked.

Henry shook his head. "I don't want to..."

Dale whirled around and slammed his hands on the arms of the wheelchair, so his face was right in Henry's.

"How did she die?" Dale yelled.

The two men glared into each other's eyes. Henry looked down first. He sighed and Dale stepped back.

"You were just a baby. She was playing down by the pond," he began, his voice trembling. "She loved that pond. Loved skipping stones across it. Playing hide and seek with your mom. But she wasn't allowed to go down there by herself."

Henry's lip quivered as the buried memories resurfaced, raw and painful.

"She snuck off while your mom was tending to you," he continued. "When your mom couldn't find her, she knew exactly where she'd run off to."

Henry took a deep breath, mustering the strength and the courage to continue.

"As soon as she stepped out of the clearing, she said she could see her yellow sundress just floating on the water. It wasn't until she got closer that she realized it was Dru.

"Your mother jumped in to save her. But it was already too late. So, she just held her. Right there on the edge of the pond. I got home later and went looking for them. She was still holding her when I found them."

He broke down, sobs wracking his body. It was the first time that Dale had ever seen his father cry.

"Your mother - she couldn't take it," he continued. "She blamed herself. I kept telling her it wasn't her fault, but she wouldn't listen. And she just drifted away. And then one day, she was just gone. Just like that."

"Why didn't you go after her?' Dale asked.

"Because someone had to take care of you!" Henry snapped, bitterness and sorrow intermingling. He took a breath. "You were just a baby. Delphine wasn't here yet. And I did look for her where I could. I called her family. I checked all the obvious places. I even told the police. But honestly, I figured she'd just come back eventually. She had you, for God's sake. Then about three months later, I got THAT letter."

He pointed at the letter Dale was holding, hating it for existing.

"I lost too much too fast," he went on. "And I had a baby boy I needed to take care of and no clue of how to do it. The only way I could cope was to just shut it all away. I figured it'd be temporary. But it just got easier to leave it all buried."

"It didn't get easier for me," Dale replied. "How did you even keep this from me?"

"I kept you at home so you never had any friends," Henry said. "And we don't really have any kin to speak of. And then I sent you off to school."

"That's going to a lot of trouble to lie to your own kid," Dale said.

"I was trying to protect you from my pain," Henry said, looking up at his son. "But I just made everything worse. I'm so sorry, Dale."

Dale was stunned. He'd never seen his father so vulnerable. And he'd never heard his father apologize.

But Dale wasn't ready to forgive just yet. He'd barely

even processed all the new information. He had questions. Lots of questions. But before he could ask the first one, the house phone rang in the kitchen. He walked into the other room to answer it.

"Hello?" he said, picking up the receiver. "Yes, this is Dale Devereux."

39

SHEETS OF RAIN fell as Dale's Jeep pulled into Virgil's driveway. Dale could see Catherine sitting in the back seat of the squad car wrapped in a blanket. The car door was open, so he assumed she wasn't being arrested. As he jumped out of the Jeep, Sergeant Wilkerson got out of the police car.

"Cat!" Dale yelled.

As he ran toward her, Wilkerson cut him off.

"Hang on," he said.

"Thanks for calling," Dale said. "She's been going through a lot lately."

"I called you, but I didn't call it in," Wilkerson said. "Dale, she's talking all kinds of nonsense."

Dale nodded.

"Thanks, Pete. She needs help," he said. "We lost a child and... it's taken a toll."

Wilkerson nodded and let Dale pass. He ran to Catherine, who was facing away, toward the woods, lost in thought.

"You okay, hon?" Dale asked.

"Dale, please. I need you to believe me," Catherine replied, still not looking at him. "I saw it all. I know it's real."

Finally, she turned to Dale.

"Please, believe me."

Dale looked into the sad, pleading eyes of his wife. He had never seen her look so unhinged.

Had she had a complete breakdown? he wondered.

The thought sent chills through Dale, and he was overrun with the fear of losing her again. He knew she needed to know the truth that he had just discovered, but he was still cautious, worried it would pull the rug out from under her too quickly.

"Come on," he said, helping her out of the car. "I need to show you something."

He thanked Wilkerson as he walked her back to the Jeep. He walked her to the passenger side but opened the back seat door. Catherine froze. Henry was sitting in the front passenger seat. He looked different to her. Weak. Broken. Ashamed.

They drove to a cemetery on the other side of town. Catherine waited while Dale helped Henry into his wheelchair and then grabbed an umbrella for Catherine. The three tried to huddle under it as Henry led them between the tombstones, scanning the inscriptions.

Then he stopped.

"Here it is," he said, his voice cracking.

They all stared at the small tombstone.

DRUCILLA DEVEREUX   MARCH 12, 1989 - JULY 18, 1995

"I barely remember the funeral," Henry said. "Everything was such a blur. Your mother was crying so hard, we had to carry her back to the car."

"She's buried here," Dale said, as much to himself as to his wife.

Catherine fell to her knees, punched in the gut. She was confused and could barely believe what she was seeing. What about the tree?

Dale stared at the marker, overwhelmed with all sorts of emotion. He wanted to feel sad, but he never knew her. Instead, he felt a familiar loneliness.

"Was I here?" he asked.

"Someone was watching you back at the house," Henry said. "You were a baby. Probably slept through the whole thing."

Dale explained to Catherine how Dru had drowned in the pond and was then discovered by her mother soon after.

"So, no one...? Catherine asked.

Dale shook his head. "She was alone. She drowned."

"I'm so sorry," Catherine said.

Dale put his hand on her shoulder.

"But it seemed so real," she said as she stood, turning to Henry. "I'm so, so sorry."

Henry reached out and squeezed her hand, forcing a weak smile.

"Me, too."

"Cat, I know you think I've been in denial about

Sarah" Dale said. "That I'm just trying to move us on. But I'm just trying to be strong for both of us. I can't lose you. You have no idea. I'm barely holding it together."

Catherine hugged him.

"I'm so sorry, Dale," she said.

"We do need to go back to the treatment center," he said. "You see that, right? This is all out of my depth."

He ran his fingers through her wet hair and could feel her nodding.

Catherine felt defeated. Humiliated. Ashamed.

Henry turned his wheelchair around and headed to the Jeep. Dale and Catherine followed slowly behind him.

40

THE HOUSE WAS BURIED in a blanket of silent sadness as Catherine packed their belongings. Dale still had his own unresolved feelings and said he needed to put gas in the car and pick up a few things. But Catherine knew he needed to be alone and process everything. He did that best while driving.

When Catherine walked downstairs to check for any clothes she had left in the laundry room, she saw Henry sitting in the parlor, staring out the window.

"You okay?" she asked quietly.

"I nearly burned that box of photos a thousand times," he said without turning to look at her. "I just could never bring myself to go through with it."

He patted his chair.

"And then I couldn't get up there to do it even if I wanted to," he said. "I considered them safely tucked away."

"I'm sorry I went snooping. I'm sorry I dredged everything up for you," she replied.

Henry hesitated before speaking.

"I'm not," he finally said. "Sometimes you bury more than the pain. It wasn't fair to Dale. None of it was."

"You were trying to protect him," Catherine offered.

Henry chuckled.

"I wish I was that noble," he said. "I was selfish. I didn't want to keep reliving it. I didn't want for it all to be real. I didn't want for them to be..."

"Gone?" Catherine finished his thought.

Henry nodded and hung his head.

"I understand that feeling," she said. "But, maybe, eventually, we have to face reality, as painful as it is."

She chuckled. "Clearly, I have not been practicing what I preach."

"Can I ask you a question?" Henry asked. "Was it Dru? That you saw? Was it really her?"

"I don't know," she said. "Maybe it's like what Dr. Mason said. That I was just missing Sarah so much. And then I saw the picture of Dru and made a connection that wasn't there... I clearly have some things I need to deal with. All I know is I'm really, really sorry."

Henry nodded, deflated. Catherine struggled for what to say.

"I should probably finish packing," Catherine said.

Henry nodded. He turned to look out the window again, watching the rain splash in the large puddles that were forming on the ground, freshly exposed after being cleared of years of neglect. He could feel years of buried sorrow rising to the surface and his heart began to break all over again. The grief poured out of him in heaving sobs.

41

CATHERINE FOLDED and rolled their clothes and stuffed them into the large green suitcase. She had already collected the toiletries from the bathroom and tossed them in several gallon freezer bags to keep them from spilling on to everything. Letting out a sigh, she scanned the room, making sure she hadn't forgotten anything.

That's when she noticed something familiar on the dresser. It was the letter from Dru's mother, no longer hidden away. Laying on top of it was the picture of Dru.

Dale must have kept them, she thought.

Catherine picked up Dru's photo and stared at it as if for the first time. She saw the little girl in the picture, not the haunting visage. But then something struck her as odd.

Dru wasn't wearing the locket that Catherine had seen in her vision. As she had replayed the previous night's visions over and over in her mind, she had assumed the locket was just something she had seen in the picture of Dru. But it wasn't there.

I'm doing it again, she thought.

She folded the letter and slipped the picture inside, sliding both in a pocket of the suitcase. But try as she might, she couldn't shake her uneasy feeling. And she knew if she didn't check on something, it would eat at her forever.

She stood at the bottom of the attic stairs, looking up into the darkness. Part of her wanted to leave well enough alone, but something stronger was pulling at her, drawing her up the steep wooden stairs.

She slowly climbed the stairs, the wood creaking under each step. As she reached into the darkness for the light's drawstring, a frigid breath of air brushed past her forearm. She jerked her hand back in fear, then took a deep breath to shake it off and bolster just enough false courage to try again. She fumbled for the string that was now swaying back and forth and quickly gave it a pull. It instantly threw a warm golden light onto the rows of boxes. Letting out a sigh of relief, Catherine continued up the stairs.

42

DR. MASON STEPPED into the parlor where Henry was still staring out the window, lost in thought. He cleared his throat to announce his presence, and Henry responded with a half-numb nod.

"I'm sorry," Dr. Mason said, running his hands through his wet hair. "I knocked, but no one answered, and the door was unlocked. It's quite a storm out there."

"I assume Dale filled you in on this morning's adventures?" Henry asked.

His voice sounded tired and resigned.

"I'm sorry you've had to be caught in the middle of all of it," Mason replied.

Using the electric controls on the arm, Henry turned his chair around with one hand. Dr. Mason noticed the glass of bourbon in the other.

"You've been drinking," he said.

"You must be loving this," Henry said. "Just another banner day in the Devereux household."

"Why don't you give me that drink, Henry," Mason said.

"Why don't you mind your own damn business?" Henry snapped back.

Mason ignored Henry and reached for the glass, but Henry jerked it away, spilling the drink everywhere. Nonplussed, Dr. Mason wrestled the glass away, and the wheelchair rolled back next to the Tiffany lamp, causing it to flicker.

"Damnit, Mason!" Henry snapped.

"Your family needs you, Henry," Mason chided. "Can you try to pull yourself together for just a little while?"

"Need me?" Henry scoffed. "They'd be better off without me."

"Don't tempt me," Mason said as he took the glass into the kitchen.

Henry calmed himself down. As he pulled away from the flickering lamp, it calmed down as well.

"I told him everything," he said loudly into the kitchen.

"Who?" Mason asked.

"Dale."

"What everything did you tell him?"

"About Dru. About Susan. About everything I had kept from him forever."

Mason rolled up the sleeves of his white dress shirt to wash the glass.

"You remember that letter she sent me?" Henry continued. "The last one?"

"The one that pushed you over the edge?" Mason asked.

"I thought I threw it away years ago, but Dale pulled it out of the trash. He's kept it all these years. Then Catherine found a picture of Dru, and it was all too much. So, I told him everything."

"I'm imagining that brought a lot back up for you," Mason said from the kitchen. "All those memories you had worked so hard to bury."

He dried his hands with a white dishtowel, then folded it over the edge of the sink before rolling his shirt sleeves back down... covering the snake tattoo on his right forearm.

43

CATHERINE SPOTTED the circle of powder from the incantation and then the scattering of photos they had pushed out of the way. She dropped to her knees and rummaged frantically through the photos, hoping to find something to confirm her theory.

She found several more of Dru. She wasn't wearing the locket in any of them. Then she found a Devereux family photo. A candid shot of the family at what looked to be a picnic. Everyone looked happy and playful. A young Henry was holding Dru's hands above her head, lifting her up to swing her back and forth. They were both laughing. Susan, Dale's mother, was also laughing as she stood next to Henry, holding an infant Dale in her arms.

Catherine squinted at the photo, trying to make out small details. It was hard to tell at first, but she was certain Dru wasn't wearing the locket in this photo either.

But Susan was.

As the realization of what she had discovered hit her,

so did a burst of cold air. It pushed her to the floor and a barrage of images filled her brain.

A man dragging something through the woods.

A heart-shaped locket falling through the air...

A snake slithering up a thorn-covered honey locust...

Dirt being shoveled over a body.

Dirt hitting the neck of a body. A neck wearing the heart-shaped locket.

Catherine sat back up, pumped with adrenaline. She scoured through the pictures, looking for more photos of Susan. There were only a few. Henry had probably destroyed all the others. But Catherine found one of Susan alone, smiling at the camera. Another of her holding an infant Dale as Dru looked up at them both fondly. One of Susan with Henry.

In every single one of them, Susan was wearing the heart-shaped locket.

The realization jolted Catherine. It was as if a curtain had been pulled back.

It all made sense now.

"It wasn't you, was it?" Catherine asked of the ghost girl she assumed was in the room. "It was your mother.'

44

HENRY STARED at the glass of water Dr. Mason had given him to replace his bourbon. He immediately gave the glass back.

"If you're going to bring me a glass, it better have bourbon in it."

"No glass it is," Mason replied. Taking the glass of water back into the kitchen.

Henry was distracted by the sounds of someone bounding down the stairs and storming into the room.

"I'm not crazy," Catherine blurted. "I just had it wrong."

Before Henry could respond, Dr. Mason walked into the room.

"Had what all wrong, dear?"

Catherine was surprised to see the doctor but not enough to dampen her enthusiasm.

"I need you both to hear me out," she said.

Dr. Mason looked at her, unsure. He looked at Henry who seemed genuinely interested.

"Please," Catherine insisted.

Dr. Mason sat down in a chair opposite Henry.

"I misinterpreted what I had seen," she continued.

"Seen where, Catherine?" Mason asked gently.

Catherine hesitated. "In my... visions."

Mason started to protest but Henry held up his hand.

"Let her talk," Henry said before turning his attention to Catherine. "What did you get wrong?"

Catherine stared into Henry's eyes, suddenly realizing the bomb she was about to drop.

"I... I don't know how to say this, Henry, but... the person I saw buried wasn't Dru. It was... your wife."

"Susan?"

Dr. Mason stood. "Oh, my poor dear. Your delusions are getting worse."

Catherine ignored him.

"I kept seeing a heart-shaped locket being covered with dirt. I just assumed it was Dru's. But I looked at other pictures I had found and..."

"That was Susan's," Henry interrupted. "I gave her that locket when Dale was born."

Henry's lip began to quiver. He shook his head. "But I don't understand."

"Catherine, this is enough," Dr. Mason said, grabbing Catherine by the arm. "Your delusions have stirred up enough painful memories for one day. Now let's get you back upstairs to lay down."

"Wait," Henry said weakly. "Are you saying someone killed Susan?"

Catherine shook herself free from Mason and knelt in front of Henry.

"I think someone killed Dru and then, to cover it up, killed Susan."

"Enough!" Mason snapped. "It's one thing for you to hurt yourself with these... these lies. But now you're dragging this poor man into it!"

"I know this all sounds crazy," Catherine said. "I thought I was crazy. But you need to believe me."

"I'm going to get you a sedative."

"But wait," Henry said. "If Susan was dead, who wrote the letter?"

"It was typewritten, right?" Catherine countered. "Anyone could have written it and forged her signature."

"Are you hearing yourself?" Mason asked. "Do you hear how ludicrous all of this sounds? These... these paranoid delusions? I'm going to get you a sedative for now, but you must promise me that, as soon as you get home, you speak to a professional immediately. I'll even call ahead."

Henry rolled his wheelchair toward the landline that sat on a shelf.

"You said you know the tree?" he asked Catherine.

"What are you doing, Henry?" Mason asked.

"I can't explain the letter, but there are too many other coincidences," Henry said. "How did Catherine know Dru died in the pond? And she said she had seen her before she ever saw a picture of her. Before she even knew she existed. And how did she know about the locket?"

"She clearly saw the locket in some of the pictures she dug up in the attic," Mason countered. "Just as she saw Dru."

"Why are you so quick to write it all off?" Henry asked.

"Because I am a doctor, and I am being reasonable. She needs help!"

Henry began to dial. "I'm calling the po–."

Before he could enter the number, Mason hit him in the back of the head with a heavy decanter. Catherine screamed as Henry fell out of his wheelchair, grabbing at Mason as he fell, ripping his sleeve and revealing his snake tattoo.

Catherine gasped in shock and terror at the tattoo. Could it be the snake from her visions? If Dru fixated on her killer's arm as it held her under, she would have stared at the image of that snake.

Dr. Mason killed Dru.

Catherine backed away. She turned to run but he grabbed her by the arm, yanking her back in the room and throwing her to the floor.

"Let's be calm, Catherine," he said, standing over her. "You're imagining things. It's all going to be okay."

He knelt beside her, holding her down. She could feel his hands slide around her neck.

"Just relax," he said. "It's going to be alright."

"Why?" she cried.

"Shhhhh."

Catherine spotted a candlestick holder that had fallen to the ground when Mason had struck Henry. She grabbed it and swung hard, hitting Mason on the side of the head and throwing him off of her. She struggled to her feet, but Mason grabbed her ankle and pulled her to the floor again.

"You killed them!" she yelled.

"I had no choice!" he argued.

Catherine turned to see a different Mason. He was filled with a rage she would never expect of him.

Catherine kicked him away and pulled herself up. Mason also stood, blocking her escape.

"We were going to run away together, but then that urchin caught us."

"So, you killed her?"

"It was an accident."

"You drowned her."

"I didn't want to kill her," he continued. "But neither one of us could afford having our affair discovered. Not until we were ready to leave. And we all know you can't trust a child to keep a secret."

Catherine grabbed a crystal vase from a shelf and threw it at him. But he caught her arm and twisted her to the ground. They rolled and knocked over the side table next to the Tiffany lamp.

Mason straddled her and began to choke her.

"I told Susan she couldn't tell anyone, and she did so good for a while, but guilt got the best of her," he said as Catherine gasped for air. "She was going to talk. To ruin everything. I didn't have a choice."

"You... always... have a... choice," Catherine muttered.

She pulled at Mason's hands, but knew she was no match.

"You should have kept your delusions to yourself," he said.

Catherine's face turned deep red, and she could feel the fight leaving her body. Everything grew blurry but then it looked as if the Tiffany lamp was flickering off and on uncontrollably.

"I warned you," Mason seethed. "Time and time again."

The Tiffany lamp toppled, shattering over Mason's head. He yelled in pain and grabbed the back of his head, releasing his grip on Catherine. She gasped in air and pushed herself free of Mason.

She crawled past Henry's body, slipping in the pool of blood that had formed around his head. He moved just enough for Catherine to know he was still alive.

Dr. Mason pushed the lamp away, pulling shards of glass out of the back of his head. As blood ran down his neck on to his white shirt, he sneered at Catherine.

"Run," Henry whispered.

Catherine struggled to her feet and staggered toward the door in the kitchen that led to the yard.

45

DALE WAS STILL ANGRY, but he had talked himself off the ledge. Yes, there was still much healing to be done but, for the first time in a long time, he felt that Catherine was finally going to be able to overcome her demons. And that he was going to resolve things with Henry. He had even bought his father groceries to keep him stocked up until they could figure out a new caregiver.

The windshield wipers slapped sheets of rainwater off of the glass, but Dale still had to squint to see through the heavy downpour. He turned off the main road and on to the private road that led to the family home. Loading up in the rain wouldn't be fun but he wasn't going to wait for it to let up. The sooner they could get out of this house the better.

~

Catherine pushed the kitchen door open and toppled out into the rain. She looked toward the driveway and could see Dale's headlights approaching. A wave of relief flooded her as she hobbled toward the lights, waving her arms over her head.

"Dale," she said, the words burning as they passed her throat, still raw from Mason's attack.

She watched as the car pulled up the circular driveway, then disappeared from sight as it neared the front door.

He can't see me in the rain, she thought as she stumbled forward, leaning against the house for support.

"Dale!" she attempted to cry out again.

The words came out stronger but were still being swallowed up in the loud storm. She prepared to let out a loud scream. But, before she could utter a sound, Mason's hand clamped over her mouth as he yanked her backwards.

Mason pulled Catherine away from the driveway and towards the path that led into the woods. Catherine screamed into his hand, flailing and kicking, but she was still too weak to fight hard. Then, Mason tripped, and they both toppled backwards into a large puddle of muddy rainwater.

They both pulled themselves up and Catherine stumbled backwards to avoid Mason's grasp. She turned to run, stumbling and falling her way down the path into the woods. Mason gathered himself and strode after her.

46

DALE SHOOK the rain off as he walked into the kitchen, setting the wet grocery bags on the counter.

"I'm back," he yelled out to anyone who could hear him. "A little wet but loaded with enough groceries to last you for quite a while."

He began to unpack the grocery bags when he heard an odd sound from the parlor.

"Hello?" he yelled out, setting the groceries down.

When no one answered, he decided to investigate. He looked into the parlor and noticed the broken Tiffany lamp.

"Everyone okay?"

His question was immediately answered when he found Henry lying on the floor, blood pooling around his head.

"Oh my God!"

He knelt next to his father, who looked up at him.

Thank God. He's conscious.

"What happened?" he asked.

"Son," Henry struggled to speak.

He squeezed Dale's hand tight and looked up at him.

"Catherine..." Henry finally said.

"What about Catherine?" Dale asked. "Where is she?"

Dale reached for the phone and dialed 9-1-1.

"Frank..." Henry muttered.

"Where's Catherine?" Dale asked again.

The 9-1-1 operator answered but before Dale could say anything, he heard a scream from the woods.

Henry managed to eek out a forceful yell. "Help her!"

Dale positioned the phone next to Henry's ear then ran toward the sounds of his wife's screams.

47

CATHERINE STUMBLED her way to the pond. She wasn't sure if she went there out of habit or if she was being drawn there. But as she neared the boathouse, Mason caught up with her.

Cornered at the water's edge, she turned to face him. His face and shirt were covered in blood and his eyes glowered in rage. He lunged at her, sending both into the water. She struggled to free herself, but he yanked her back by the hair, pushing her under.

She thrashed frantically, trying to break free from his grasp. But he was too strong, and she could slowly feel the fight leaving her body. She became filled with a sense of empty hopelessness. It almost felt as if it were in slow motion as she looked up at Dr. Mason grimacing down at her. As she began to lose consciousness, she saw the maniacal look in his eyes. And she found herself fixating on the snake tattoo on his forearm.

She began to wonder if the visions she had seen were not of Mason killing Dru, but a premonition of Mason drowning her. Had she witnessed her future death? Or was it the same death? One vision shared across two victims?

No! She thought. *I won't be his victim!*

She summoned every remaining ounce of strength she had and reached up to grab Mason by the hair and yank him downward under water.

Now they both struggled underwater, each not relenting. But then they were joined by another figure. Catherine recognized her immediately. It was the ghastly, decayed corpse of Dru. Mason turned to see what Catherine was looking at and shrieked back in terror. Dru stared directly into her killer's face. Then she smiled. An evil, malevolent smile. She quickly placed a hand over Mason's face and pushed him under her.

Mason yelled in terror, letting go of Catherine. She pulled herself to the surface, gasping for air. She backed away toward the shore as Mason thrashed violently underwater. Dale burst through the woods and rushed over to his wife, sliding to his knees and helping her out of the water. He held her as she coughed and gasped and they both watched as Mason struggled underwater.

Dale started to rush in and save the doctor, but Catherine held him back. They both watched as Mason's weak, unmoving body was lifted out of the water by someone. Dale couldn't believe what he was seeing.

It was a gray, decayed corpse of a young girl. Even though he couldn't recognize her, he somehow sensed it was his sister. He watched in shock and horror as Dru lifted Mason's weak body up high then slammed it into the water. She then dove in, pulling Mason under with her. The fighting stopped and the water instantly stilled to a mirror calm. As Dale and Catherine watched, Mason's lifeless body floated to the surface, face down.

Dale held Catherine tight, staring at the body, trying to piece together everything he had just seen. A rustle in the bushes caught their attention and they both turned to see Virgil standing behind the bushes. He had seen the entire thing.

48

An hour later, the storm had passed, and the Devereux property was swarming with police officers and EMTs. Henry, his head bandaged, lay in a gurney in the back of an ambulance, tormenting a paramedic with his cranky personality.

The pond was also swarmed with law enforcement. Even though Mason's body had been pulled from the water, forensics specialists waded in the pond, looking to see what had held Mason under. Catherine, wrapped in a blanket and sitting up on a hill with Dale, was smart enough not to tell the police that a ghost had drowned Mason. Instead, she told them that Mason had been trying to drown her and, in the struggle, had got himself tangled or pinned underwater. It was a version corroborated by Dale.

Virgil also told a similar story. Catherine wasn't sure if he had also decided it was best not to bring up a ghost or that he just hadn't seen Dru. Either way, he was a witness that saw Mason drag Catherine into the water to drown her and no one else was there.

Sergeant Wilkerson told Dale that his father was going to be alright. He had lost a lot of blood, but probably only suffered a concussion and needed a few stitches.

"If anything, he's stunned by everything," Wilkerson said. "I mean, can you imagine finding out one of your oldest friends had not only had an affair with your wife, but killed her and your daughter?"

As the two men talked, Catherine looked out over the water, still trying to make sense of everything that had happened. As she absent-mindedly surveyed the area, she began to hear the whispers again. She looked around frantically. Something in the woods caught her attention. She wasn't sure what it was, but she knew she had to investigate. Without saying a word, she dropped the blanket and started to walking toward the woods.

Wilkerson yelled at her to come back, but Dale stopped him. Instead, the two men followed at a safe distance behind her.

Catherine walked into the woods, which grew thicker and darker with every step. The whispers had morphed into the familiar humming of a child's song. Something caught her attention again. But this time, Catherine knew with absolute certainty what it was. Dru stood in the distance, looking healthy and wearing her bright yellow dress. She smiled at Catherine, making sure she had been seen before skipping further into the woods.

Catherine picked up her pace to keep up with the glimpses of Dru. Dale and Wilkerson followed suit. She charged deep into the thicket. Brush and vines slapped against her arms and legs. Finally, she spotted a flash of yellow up ahead. She ran toward it then saw something that made her stop in her tracks. At the same moment, the humming stopped.

It was the tree with thorny spikes.

Catherine ran to the tree and placed her hand on the bark just as Dale and Wilkerson caught up with her. They watched as Catherine dropped to her knees and started to dig.

"Sweetheart," Dale said gently as he walked up to her. "What are you doing?"

Catherine didn't answer but kept swiping dirt away. Dale knelt beside her.

"Cat?" he said calmly.

Then Catherine stopped. She felt something. She began to brush the dirt away to reveal a hint of red fabric and a glint of metal. She dug a little more and pulled out something.

A heart-shaped locket.

Catherine held it out in front of Dale.

"Dale," Catherine said quietly. "This was your mother's."

Dale took the locket and opened it. Inside was a still-intact baby picture of himself on one side and a picture of Dru on the other. He stared in shock and disbelief, overwhelmed with so many conflicting emotions.

"She didn't leave you," Catherine said.

Dale looked at her, too puzzled, confused and disoriented to even ask a question. They were interrupted by Wilkerson who walked in between them.

"What have you got?" he asked the couple.

"There's a body buried here," Catherine said, looking at Dale. "Susan Devereux's body."

Wilkerson reached down to wipe away more dirt until he spotted something he recognized.

"Holy shit," he muttered. "We've got bones."

He stood up and yelled back toward the police.

"We've got bones!"

The police officer pulled Catherine and Dale away from the tree and the couple watched as police and forensics specialists swarmed the tree with shovels. Catherine turned to Dale.

"I'm sorry," she said.

Dale looked at her, tears welling up in his eyes. He nodded gently, and, as the truth sunk in, he offered a gentle smile.

"I wasn't crazy," she said.

He nodded.

"No," he replied. "You weren't."

Two days later.

Catherine hammered a nail into the parlor wall and hung a picture frame. She stood back to admire her handiwork just as Dale walked into the room.

"His majesty is asking that you please stop hammering," Dale said before turning to look at the picture. "Oh, wow."

Dale took a step toward it, taking in the family portrait of Henry, Susan, Dru and an infant Dale.

"Is it okay? Too much? Too soon?"

Dale stared at the family he never even knew existed. "It's great," he replied.

"You think Henry will mind?"

"He'll never admit he likes it. He'll probably even complain about it. About where you put it. About the frame. But trust me. He'll love it."

Catherine smiled.

"How's he doing?" Catherine asked.

"He's kind of in a state of shock. I mean, there's a part of him that feels relieved that his wife didn't leave him. On the other hand, it was because she was murdered. And that his daughter was murdered. And an affair. And all by someone he trusted. It's a lot to take in."

"How are you doing with it all?" she asked.

Dale sighed. "To be honest, I'm not even sure if I've completely wrapped my head around it. I'm honestly shell-shocked. And then there's the whole ghost thing."

"But you believe me, right?"

Dale shrugged. "I can't come up with a better explanation for all of it."

He turned from the photo, wanting to change the subject.

Oh, I spoke to the police again today."

"Again?"

"No big deal. Just to catch us up on everything. They met with Virgil again. Just to double-check his statement. And get this. He told them that he had seen Doc drown Dru. And my mom was right there. Just like you said."

"Why did he never say anything?" Catherine asked.

"His mother wouldn't let him. Told him it was none of his business and the police wouldn't believe him. Would blame him. She really did a number on him."

"Is he going to get in trouble?" Catherine asked. "Withholding evidence or something?"

"I don't think so," Dale replied. "Given Virgil's mental state."

He paused before continuing.

"Honey, I'm really sorry you didn't feel like you could talk to me about all of this."

Catherine turned, surprised for the sudden shift in the conversation.

"Dale, it's okay."

"I would have believed you."

Catherine gave him a knowing smile.

"No, you wouldn't have. But that's okay. I wouldn't have believed me, either."

Dale smiled back and then hesitated before speaking again.

"Are you upset? That it wasn't... Sarah?"

The name sent a surge of pain through Catherine's body. She let out a quivering sigh and collected herself.

"I was. At first," she said. "But maybe it's okay. Maybe that means she's at peace. At least that's what I want to believe."

Dale reached out and squeezed her hand.

"I can't say it enough but I'm sorry I've been so closed off about... everything."

Catherine nodded in response.

"I miss her," Dale said. "But I'm afraid of the pain."

A tear rolled down his cheek and he quickly wiped it away.

"I don't think it will ever go away," Catherine said. "I think, at best, we'll just get used to it. Find a way to live with it."

"I don't know if I can," Dale said.

"I don't either," she replied. "But we have to try. Together."

The couple shared a gentle kiss and held each other

until a bell began to ring. Dale groaned as he pulled away.

"If we can survive Henry," he said.

"You go on and check on him," she said. "I really want to get this place back in shape before he's up and about."

"Just hold off on the hammering for a bit," Dale said with a light smile.

She gave him a peck on the cheek and began to pick up some of the photos scattered around the room.

"You know," she said. "This clean-up would go a lot faster if Delphine was still here."

Dale laughed. "That woman could clean like it was nobody's business."

They both put the photos into a box, but Dale stopped and turned to Catherine.

"Wait. How do you know about Delphine?"

Catherine smiled at him, assuming he was teasing, but then saw the confused look on his face.

"What do you mean 'how do I know about her'?" Catherine asked.

"Did Henry tell you about her?" Dale asked.

"Hon, you're not making any sense. She's only been gone a couple of days."

Dale turned white.

"Wait. Are you saying you saw Delphine? Here?"

"You're not making any sense," Catherine replied, clearly confused.

Dale frantically rummaged through the box of photos until he found what he was looking for. He handed the photo to Catherine. It was of Delphine with toddler Dale and younger Henry.

"This Delphine," Dale said.

"Yes," Catherine replied. "Dale, what are you…"

But then she noticed something odd about the photo. While Dale and Henry were considerably younger, the Delphine in the photo looked the same age as the Delphine she had known.

"Delphine came on to help around the house when I was still a baby," Dale explained. "But, honey, she died more than ten years ago."

All the color drained from Catherine's face. She could feel her knees getting weak.

"That can't be."

She sat down, stunned. "I swear. It was her."

Dale brushed her hair with his fingers.

"She was right here," she muttered.

"Holy shit," Dale whispered. "You saw her, too. Didn't you?"

Catherine nodded slowly, trying to absorb the truth. The moment was broken by yet another bell ring. Dale let out a sigh.

"I'll be right back," he said.

Catherine grabbed his wrist as he walked away.

"Dale," she asked, her voice quivering. "You believe me, don't you?"

Dale cupped her face in his hands and kissed her forehead.

"I do," he said. "I don't understand it. But I do believe you."

The bell rang again.

"I'll be right back. You need to tell me everything."

As he walked away, Catherine stared at the picture of

Delphine and began to replay every encounter she had had with her, seeing it all very differently.

No one else ever interacted with her.

No one else ever spoke to her.

No one else even seemed to acknowledge her.

She knew the way to the other side, because she was already there. She was here to guide me. And keep me sane.

"Thank you," Catherine whispered to the empty room.

Something outside caught her attention. Near the rear of the yard, a shadow moved between the bushes. Catherine's heart skipped a beat, and she walked to the window, just in time to see a squirrel scurry from the bushes into a tree.

She let out a sigh of relief, then slowly lowered the blinds.

Thank you for reading
THE GIRL IN THE WHISPERS

If you enjoyed it, please leave a review on Amazon.com or Goodreads, or wherever you purchased your copy. A review can go a long way in helping other readers find this book.

.

Don't miss these other books by
David K. Wilson

SAM LAWSON MYSTERY SERIES
"Sam goes down like a smooth glass of whisky."
COMBUSTIBLE
BENEATH THE SURFACE
DARK HARBOR
DEADLY REPUTATION
DEATH ON LOCATION
BEFORE HER LAST BREATH
MURDER IN SPA CITY

ALSO AVAILABLE:
RED DIRT BLUES
"Wildly entertaining and absurdly funny."

GET A FREE COPY OF *BOUND BY MURDER*
This fun and riveting mystery novella e-book is available
for free at **davidkwilsonauthor.com**

ACKNOWLEDGMENTS

As always, there are so many people that had a hand in bringing *The Girl In The Whispers* to life, including Shelley Upchurch, Yvonne Pelletier, James Hewitson, Barbara Fournier and Lorraine Evanoff.

MVP awards go to Rena Grubbs and Regina Riddle, who were subjected to multiple readings of the manuscript as I worked through rewrites.

A special thank you to Jo-Ann Lant, who is not only my unofficial publicist, but also my hilarious Facebook Live co-host.

And a shout-out to my two youngest (but still adult) children Colin and Mallory, whose love of horror served as both inspiration and a source for advice.

Finally, a big hug to my family of fellow authors who have created a sense of community in what can often be a very solitary endeavor. Thanks for your support and friendship.

ABOUT THE AUTHOR

David K. Wilson is the author of the popular Sam Lawson Mystery series and the highly lauded crime comedy, *Red Dirt Blues*. He is also a seasoned ghostwriter and screenwriter. David grew up in East Texas, spent twenty years in Chicago, and currently lives in upstate New York.

Sign up to receive updates on David's future novels at
davidkwilsonauthor.com.

facebook.com/davidkwilsonauthor

instagram.com/davidkwilsonauthor

goodreads.com/davidkwilson

Made in the USA
Las Vegas, NV
22 November 2024

12389189R00135